WHEREVER SHE GOES

PSYCHIC SEASONS
BOOK FOUR

REGINA WELLING

D1733325

Wherever She Goes

Copyright © 2012 by ReGina Welling

ISBN-9781511966528

Cover design by: L. Vryhof

http://reginawelling.com

First Edition

Printed in the U.S.A.

Table of Contents

Dedication

This book, in fact, this entire series, is dedicated to my friends and family for their unfailing support.

I love you all. This is for you.

CHAPTER ONE

In the space between one breath and the next, the music stopped, everything slowed, and the only thing Kathleen Canton could hear was the sound of her own heartbeat as she gazed into eyes the color of melted chocolate. She blinked, then blinked again, but nothing changed.

She could still see him.

Feet dragging, she tried to keep dancing. The music faded to a buzzing noise that vibrated through her head in waves while she fought against panic to take the next breath. Her heart lurched in her chest and then started to race, each beat sounding like a metronome. Face tingling, Kat felt it when the world began to tunnel into the fading distance and caught herself just on the brink of fainting in Zack Roman's arms.

Another hour, Zack thought. Just one more hour, and then he could slide out the door, go home, and get out of this monkey suit. He glanced around the room, alert to that vague tingle that always warned him of trouble. Sworn to protect and serve, he wore the mantle of responsibility 24/7.

Satisfied all was as it should be, he turned his attention back to the woman in his arms and realized the source of that tingle had been right here all along. Her annoyance was an electric thing, pulsing and sparking at him.

Nothing like anger to bring out the best in a woman. Like right now, for instance. Head thrown back, shoulders squared off, she prepared to take him down a peg or two. She opened that gorgeous mouth to treat him to a scathing retort for his ill-timed comment about her psychic ability, then snapped it shut again and turned her head away.

Just about to ask her if something was wrong, he felt her body loosen up as, with a sigh, she lowered her head to rest on his shoulder.

Something was wrong. His cop sense screamed it, and he instinctively gathered her closer. Bending his head to see if he could get a closer look, he inhaled deeply when the scent of her rose up to tickle against his nose. Zack did his best to ignore the spark of interest that flared in him and instead tightened strong arms around her and slowed his steps to give her a chance to regain her composure.

A deluge of thoughts raced through Kat's mind, but only one seemed to be blinking neon. I can see, I can see, I can see.

But why now? Did it have something to do with Zack?

Kat was overwhelmed with the urge to laugh and cry at the same time. She wanted to shout from the rooftops that her vision had returned. But what if it didn't last? Just in case, she'd better keep quiet. No sense in jinxing herself.

Yes, that would be the best thing. Decision made, she carefully smoothed away the shocked expression on her now pale face and lifted her head again. Fixing her eyes straight ahead, she searched her memory for the topic and then picked up the discussion where they had left off.

"You don't believe in the supernatural." It was more a statement than a question; to her surprise, Zack seemed unaware that anything momentous had happened.

"In what? Ghosts and crystal balls and 'I see dead people'?" Zack scoffed.

"What about intuition? Do you believe in that?" Dealing with skeptics went along with the territory when you made a living reading cards and connecting people with the other side.

She had him there. His "cop sense," as he called it, was legendary. Or it had been until Logan Ellis came along, and there it had failed him miserably. The man had managed to elude arrest ever since Zack's sister, Gustavia, had helped expose the con Ellis had been trying to run on her best friend, Julie.

In fact, Zack had only agreed to attend this wedding on the off chance that Ellis might be crazy or stupid enough to try and sneak in while his ex-fiancé was getting married.

"I follow my gut if that's what you're asking, but that's instinct—finely honed instinct. It doesn't come from spirits or the ether; it comes from paying attention to body language and subtle clues. It's a skill."

"A skill you developed from nothing or one you were born with and honed over the years?"

Kat already knew the truth just as surely as she could predict his answer. Yet she waited for his confirmation. Most people as intuitive as Zack were born with a heightened level of psychic ability—not on Kat's level usually—but high enough to notice if they wanted to admit to it.

"I have always had a knack for finding things, people, whatever. Let's not make more of it than it is."

"And I have a knack for talking to dead people. Let's not make less of that than it is." Kat refused to be dismissed, "It's not a lifestyle choice or a fad or a party trick." There was a trace of bitterness in how she spat out each word. "It's a gift."

That it was a gift she would prefer to return was her own business and none of his.

Continuing this conversation seemed like a waste of time. There was nothing she could say to change his mind; if there were, a tow truck couldn't drag it out of her. Over the years, she'd learned the most combative of skeptics were often those who most wanted to believe. Unable to ask outright for a reading, they tried to goad her into providing proof that the spirit world existed.

Determined not to let Zack get past her defenses, Kat just kept dancing to what must have been the longest song ever written and tried to ignore the fact that just being near him made her nervous.

By choice, her experience with men had been limited to little more than the casual contact that came from reading their cards or contacting lost loved ones.

"You're not going to go into some kind of trance and connect with one of my old grannies to prove a point, are you?"

And there it is, she thought. The not-very-subtle bid for proof.

Then, despite vowing to herself that she would keep quiet, Kat heard herself say, "Certainly not. But, if you send someone out to Shanahan's barn, you'll find the hockey equipment stolen from the school the day before winter break." She felt his jolt of surprise through the fingers that rested lightly on his shoulder. "Up in the loft, look for two bags covered with hay."

Surprise brought his feet to a stop. Kat got one last dig in, "And, what's more, it wasn't the Shanahan boy who put the stuff there. When you find it—and you will—make sure you talk to the younger sister."

She continued when he didn't speak, "or you can assume I'm

just playing you and keep blaming it on the Hastings brothers. Now that the song has ended, I want to return to my seat.

Without another word, he guided her to the head table, where she hoped to spend a moment or two alone with her thoughts.

As he walked away, her vision dimmed but stopped short of fading to total blackness. Ironic, really, she thought, that fear of seeing ghosts caused my blindness, and now everyone looks ghostly.

Still, it was an improvement, and the timing confirmed that proximity to Zack played a part in the change. Kat sighed. Getting her vision back should make her life less complicated, not more.

The background of wedding sounds, rustling dresses, happy laughter, and music were a distraction from the volume of spirits vying for her attention. For this reason, Kat found it easier to avoid large crowds. Family members understandably wanted to contact their non-living loved ones when they saw an opportunity, whether it was appropriate to the occasion or not. A wedding was not the time to approach a skeptic with the knowledge that the spirit of his dog was barking around her ankles or even to reassure a mother that her son was safe and happy on the other side.

Moreover, being blind complicated any method she could use to provide those connections with any dignity. Yelling out names to the crowd or having someone guide her around the room and—well—that was a spectacle she refused to create. Of course, given what had just happened, that might all be about to change.

So why wasn't she more excited? She'd been able to see clearly without having to channel Estelle. That was huge.

Amazing.

But—and it was a big but—it had involved close proximity to the major complication named Zack Roman.

CHAPTER TWO

With Kat safely escorted to her table, Zack stepped outside. He needed a moment to cool off and maybe make a phone call. Or not.

Did he really want to know if that hockey equipment was concealed in Shanahan's barn? If it was, he might have to change his dinner order for the reception and have the crow entree. And, if it wasn't—well, he would be right. Nothing wrong with that.

Nothing except some small part of him wanted her to be right. Not because he wanted to believe she actually was psychic but because she seemed to fit perfectly in his arms while they were dancing. She smelled nice. Not flowery. Fresh like a summer day. And when was the last time he had noticed how a woman smelled?

The late December chill initially felt nice after the warmth and closeness created by the wedding guests inside. Zack preferred smaller crowds—less jangling to the nerves. Any large group of people automatically put him on alert. Watchful for any signs of trouble.

Thankfully, the guests at this wedding seemed well-behaved, though the night was still young, so he intended to reserve judgment on that.

Once the brisk wind had blown away the last remnants of party-generated heat, Zack stepped back into a more sheltered area of the porch, pulled out his phone, and with a few terse words, sent a deputy on what he assumed was an expedition in search of the undomesticated goose.

On the one hand, it would be nice to find the equipment and put an end to the mystery. On the other, he had a distinct mental image of picking his way across a floor littered with the worms that would surely have flown out of the can he would have opened by depending on a psychic prediction.

Either way, in half an hour or less, he would know. Whichever way it went—goose or crow—he would own it. That was his job and the way he chose to live his life.

Zack slipped back inside while shrugging off the tiny voice in the back of his mind that kept insisting he could dance with her some more if she were right.

Twenty minutes later, Zack was thankful when his phone rang. Somehow, he had gotten caught up in a conversation with Tyler's great aunt Tilly that involved his looking at numerous pictures of her latest grandson.

"Sorry, official business, I need to take this." He breathed a sigh of relief and slipped back outside to the frigid porch.

"Roman's famous gut strikes again. It was all there, right where you said it would be—and get this—the daughter was the culprit, not the Shanahan boy. Says she was mad because Coach wouldn't let her on the team. The girl was already having second thoughts and planned to return everything before the storm hit, and then it was too late. You want me to take her in or let the principal and her folks hash it out?"

"Give Slater a call; see if he wants to press charges. I'd bet he won't. What does your gut tell you about her? Does she need more?"

"Nah, she's a good kid who got mad enough to do something stupid, then regretted it immediately and tried to make it right before anyone noticed. My instincts say she's not a troublemaker, and it was just an impulsive act."

"Okay. I'll let you take care of it and get back to the party."

Zack hung up but did not return to the reception right away. He needed to think over what he was going to say to Kat. There must be some diplomatic way to save face while admitting he had been wrong. Too bad nothing came to mind.

Unless she'd had inside knowledge and used it for gain. But what would be the benefit of that? Pacing to keep warm, steam from his breath clouded the air as Zack huffed his way to a conclusion.

No benefit at all.

Kat had asked for nothing in return for the information—neither money nor admiration. Her tone of voice had made the latter quite clear. Accusing one of her best friends of colluding with a criminal would not win him any points with Gustavia either.

Nevertheless, it was the only thing that made any sense.

A white gust of frozen breath plumed from his nose while Zack paced. Since twenty more measured steps back and forth across the porch had changed nothing, Zack swung the big door open and stalked back to where Kat sat quietly amid the celebration.

She heard him coming—the slap of each footfall, sure and purposeful, mingled in with the sounds of dancing but was still distinct enough for her to pick up their cadence. She smelled him before he got close—subtle cologne mixed with soap and the cold scent of winter. That last sent a shot of tension up her spine. Was there trouble? Had Logan returned?

Julius, resident ghost and great-grandfather to the bride, had been tracking Julie's ex-fiancé for the past few days and assured them that Logan was well away and not in a position to cause trouble at the wedding. Still, she reached out to Julius with just a tendril of thought.

"All is well," was the faint reply. Kat breathed a sigh of relief before lifting her head toward where Zack loomed over.

"How did you know?" His voice sounded like steel coated with a thick layer of scorn. Gradually, everything around her came again into focus. Now she had no doubt her returning vision was somehow tied to him.

"I could answer, but we both already know the explanation will make you cranky."

He snorted. Cranky?

For some reason, the snort amused Kat. Instead of treating him to a scathing retort, she let her smirk tell the tale and was rewarded with a groan of frustration.

"Did someone tell you? The girl?" There were limits to her patience, which he was pushing past with all the finesse of a bulldozer.

Now that she could take a closer look at him, there was some small amount of pleasure in seeing the frustrated expression on his handsome face. Eyes that could crinkle when he laughed but go hard and flat when he went into cop mode blazed with indignation—one eyebrow raised as he anticipated her answer. Of course, he did not want to hear what she had to say.

"Sure," she infused the word with sarcasm. "That must be it because I'm a hack, a charlatan. Psychic confessor to confused adolescents everywhere. I see all. I know all. Come. Tell me your secrets, and I'll rat you out to the cops the first chance I get. Keeps the clients coming back, and you know I can't think of anything more fun than taking allowance money from thirteen-year-old girls. You can't see it, but in my head, I'm presenting you with a rude hand gesture that is greatly inappropriate for a wedding."

"If it wasn't the girl, then the mother?"

"That gesture? With both hands and before you ask, it wasn't her brother, or her father, or the family dog."

"Then how?" Zack settled in the chair beside her and gentled his voice while maintaining a sense of skepticism, which did not fool Kat.

Kat countered, "How does your "cop sense" work?"

Her question surprised him into an effort to articulate the experience, something he had never done before.

"I'm not sure I can explain."

"Try me." The words dropped from her lips as dry as desert sand.

"There's no voice in my head, no spirit whispering in my ear. I look at the evidence, talk to the victims, the suspects, read the reports, and get a tingle, see the pattern, the balance."

"Tingle?"

"When all the pieces of a case slide into place, it just..it feels right. Until then, I am compelled to keep looking. Nothing psychic, just my instincts."

"And your instincts about me? What are they telling you?" Kat was curious.

"That you don't lie," he admitted.

"Trust your gut," and hearing the unmistakable sounds of Gustavia making her way to the table, that was the last she said on the subject before being whisked away to perform bridesmaid duties.

CHAPTER THREE

Back in her room, Kat shucked off the bridesmaid dress and pulled on probably the rattiest pair of sweatpants in the world. Getting the pins out of her hair took her comfort level up another notch, and she happily rubbed her nails over a few spots where the updo had pulled against her scalp, then went into the bathroom to scrub off the makeup.

Finally, feeling more like herself than she had all day, Kat switched on the gas fireplace, huddled on the sofa with her knees drawn up to her chest, and began to sort through the thoughts and impressions that threatened to overwhelm her.

Julie had been a radiant, beautiful bride. Channeling Estelle's thoughts and feelings had only enhanced her own emotions at having the privilege of seeing Julie and Tyler speak their vows. Kat got a bit teary just thinking about it again.

Being in a large group of people was something Kat found exhausting on both a spiritual and physical level. She often had to fight to keep her expression from reflecting things that spirit whispered in her ear. Just tonight, for instance, Tyler's great-grandmother had told her a story about a nephew who just happened to be attending the wedding, a camp outhouse, and a handful of firecrackers that was hilariously inappropriate. All while she was being introduced to the man in question.

She'd just congratulated herself for getting through the experience without triggering any verbal landmines when Gustavia had practically forced Zack to dance with her. He had said something that made her instinctively turn her face up to his, and BAM, her life had been turned upside down again, and now she had questions. Questions that may not have answers and no one available to ask—unless…

"Estelle?" Kat whispered into the darkness, hoping Julie's grandmother's spirit had had enough time to regenerate just enough energy to communicate.

"Here," came the faint reply though Kat sensed the spirit harbored some reluctance about addressing the topic she knew Kat would be raising.

"Do you know what happened tonight?"

"Yes. Blue eyes met brown."

"But, it only lasted a little while, then everything faded back to black. I thought…I mean…was it just a passing thing?" The hope she had felt in those moments of clear vision now felt as substantial as a puff of smoke. Until it was gone, she hadn't known how strongly that hope had built inside her.

"Or will I only be able to see if he is in the room?" Please let that not be the case. He seemed nice enough, and looking at him was no hardship. Tall but not lanky, honey blond hair, expressive brown eyes that could go from warm to flat in an instant, kissable lips, and an adorable little cleft in his chin.

Still, when Estelle had said she would regain her sight, she had assumed the effect would not be conditional on his presence. Now she felt all churned up inside.

"Have faith, young Kathleen. That it happened once should

generate confidence that it will happen again. Be your own catalyst." Estelle's voice faded from Kat's mind.

Instead of answers, Kat was now left with more questions. Why did spirits always feel the need to be cagey? All this subterfuge was beyond annoying.

When she finally climbed into it, the bed felt warm and inviting, but sleep did not come easily, and when it did, it brought a series of dreams that left Kat unsettled.

She woke several times during the night to touch the button on her talking alarm clock, thinking it must be nearly morning, only to find that a bare handful of minutes had passed. Each time, a softly slurred whisper faded as she came awake. The muted voice wasn't distinct enough to make out words, but she thought she heard, "I'm sorry." It could have been an odd wind flirting with the eaves or an actual voice speaking to her nearly every night.

Eventually, unseen by Kat, a beautiful sunrise was nearing the peak of its colors when the tiredness of her body finally pulled her mind under, and she slept dreamlessly until mid-morning.

With a cup of tea held in both hands, Gustavia sat at the kitchen table and watched Fritzie and Lola out the window. The dogs raced and played in the mounded snow liberally blanketing the backyard of Hayward House, her temporary home. The sight of the much larger Lola letting little bitty Fritzie break a trail to their favorite stand of bushes brought a smile to her face.

Fritzie might be on the large side for a Jack Russell terrier, but it seemed no one had ever sent him the memo that he was not Lola-sized, so even though the boxer towered over the smaller dog, he was always the leader of the pack.

Since neither dog loved wallowing through deep snow, they

quickly did their business and raced back toward the deck. Gustavia hurried to open the sliding glass door just in time for both dogs to flash past her in a flurry of cold air and flying snow.

The two dogs made a quick circuit around the room to sniff out whether anything had changed during their brief time outside, then settled down on the floor around Gustavia's feet.

Hayward House had been passed down to Julie, but her great-grandfather Julius had had the biggest impact on the place. An inventor, one of his works made a small fortune, some of which he spent putting his unique stamp on his home.

By the time he was finished, both wings of his once-perfect example of a large Greek revival home had been modified to add Gothic buttresses and spired rooflines. For the interior, he had wheeled deals with the owner of a large furniture store and a prominent designer. He gave them carte blanch to decorate the bedrooms and other living areas in a variety of styles and take photographs for their brochures and other publicity purposes.

As a result, every one of the bedroom suites was tightly themed. Rococo, Art Deco, American Craftsman, and more. At one point, the house had been used as a boarding home for war-widowed women. Eventually, to save on maintenance, most of the furniture had been piled into a couple of large storage areas, and parts of the house had been closed up. Over the past few months, Julie and Tyler had been systematically restoring the suites to serve as backdrops for the fashion photography that was quickly becoming Julie's stock in trade.

Convinced that his ne'er do well son would squander everything passed down to him, Julius devised a complicated series of clues as a treasure hunt he felt only a worthy descendant could solve. Then, he'd promptly died before passing those clues on to his next of kin.

By the time Julie ended up sole owner, Hayward House desperately needed windows and a new roof, and she was playing beat the clock to come up with the money for the repairs.

When Gustavia had dragged Julie off to see Kat for a Tarot reading last spring, Julius and Estelle had used the psychic medium to reconnect with their granddaughter, provide her with those clues and a warning about Logan Ellis, to whom she had recently become engaged.

Less than a year later, Julie had shaken off that vile con man of a fiancé and married Tyler Kingsley, the love of her life. Three of the four caches Julius had hidden were already found, and Hayward House sat safely under its new roof.

It hadn't been only Julie's life that changed, either. Gustavia had met a long-lost aunt, reunited with her family, and found Finn—the man she hoped to start a new family with someday. Of course, she had also been targeted and kidnapped by Julie's crazy ex, who blamed her for every bad thing that had happened to him.

That's how she ended up living here—temporarily—at Hayward House. After banding together to pull off a spectacular rescue mission led by Amethyst and her tracking abilities, the little group of friends had all gotten together and decided it wasn't safe for Gustavia to live alone in her little cottage home. And much as she hated to admit it, they were probably right. Logan had grabbed her in broad daylight from a public place, and she did feel more protected now, even if she missed being in her own space.

Kat felt the same way, Gustavia knew, because they'd talked about it. Still, the psychic had also been installed in a lovely suite of rooms here because, being blind, she was doubly vulnerable if Logan ever decided to set his sights on anyone other than Julie and Gustavia.

With a sigh, Gustavia moved around the kitchen, tidying up. Content to leave the rest of the house alone, Estelle had redecorated only two rooms turning one into a studio space and updating the kitchen, which now carried a heavy sixties vibe mixed with a bit of farmhouse flair.

Estelle had left the brick fireplace area and the heavy oak trestle table that took up one end of the room and went perfectly with the still-existing slate sink that spanned a four-foot wide area under the window. Everything else had received a face-lift.

Most of the budget had gone into installing new appliances, the rest into replacing doors and drawer fronts, resulting in a dazzling blend of clean white cabinetry set off by a range, double wall oven, and refrigerator in blush pink.

The finished room was so totally Estelle that Gustavia could still picture the tiny woman's birdlike movements as she baked a batch of light and fluffy biscuits. In the short time she'd known Grams—Estelle insisted on the nickname—Gustavia had soaked up every bit of knowledge she could about cooking and running a home.

A batch of those biscuits currently baked in the top oven while the scent of a perfectly constructed frittata wafted from the bottom.

Lola perked up just before Gustavia heard the sound of footsteps on the upstairs landing. Kat must have been tired after the wedding celebration because she rarely slept this late. Gustavia couldn't help but smile as Lola dashed from the room with her usual graceless abandon the minute she heard the first step on the stair.

From day one, the big dog had taken a liking to the blind woman and felt it was her duty to play guide. Right now, she would be at Kat's side, using her body to nudge a change of direction around any barrier she perceived might be a problem.

Knowing her friend's preferences, Gustavia reached over and punched the button on the coffeemaker. Kat would drink tea, but given the option, she preferred coffee. And from the look of her this morning, probably a double shot.

"Bad dreams?" Gustavia asked with concern after studying the shadows under Kat's eyes, so dark they stood out in her pale face.

Voice dry, Kat replied, "You'd have to sleep to have dreams."

Counting her steps as always, Kat slid into a chair and leaned an elbow on the table to rest her head against her hand.

"Want to tell me about it?" Gustavia placed a warm hand over Kat's where it lay on the table. A bubbling gurgle preceded the coffee maker's beeping to let them know the pot was finished brewing. Kat started to rise, but Gustavia insisted, "I'll pour you a cup. I need to check on breakfast anyway," and went to pick out a novelty mug with *all the coffee in the world won't make me a morning person* printed on it. "Want me to fix you a plate?"

Kat had that echoing hollow feeling in the pit of her stomach, the one that always followed a night without sleep. Maybe some food would ease the clawing ache.

"Smells good in here, biscuits and something egg-based?"

"Nail on the head. Frittata with mushrooms and peppers." Gustavia set the coffee down next to Kat's hand and placed the sugar bowl and creamer nearby, knowing that the sound of the dishes making contact with the table would be enough of a guide for Kat to find them easily.

Then, with one eye on Kat, she bustled around the kitchen grabbing plates and setting food on the table while leaving some in the oven to stay warm for Julie and Tyler.

Throughout the meal, Kat's pallor improved, her normally rosy cheeks regaining enough of their color that Gustavia felt it was time to ask.

"Do you want to tell me what happened?"

"While dancing with your brother, I got my sight back for a little while." The words were softly spoken—almost apologetic.

"But that's great news." Gustavia couldn't understand why Kat wasn't doing cartwheels. Okay, so cartwheels might not be the best idea for a blind woman to be doing in an enclosed space, but dejection instead of elation seemed all kinds of wrong. "Isn't it?"

"Did you miss the two main points? *Dancing with your brother* and *for a little while*."

"Ah, okay. It's the *blue eyes meets brown* thing that's bothering you?"

"A bit," came the sarcastic lilt, "I don't even know Zack, so why him? Why now?"

"Did you talk to Estelle?"

"*Be your own catalyst*. That's what she said. What's that supposed to mean?"

Gustavia could tell that Kat really just wanted support, not an honest opinion, so she made a noncommittal noise and listened to the mild rant.

"If it happened once, it can happen again." Kat singsonged in an exaggerated mimic of Estelle's other piece of advice while Gustavia refilled her mug and tried to stifle a snort of amusement, which she—quite rightly—assumed would not be welcome at the moment.

"I'll admit I am surprised at it being my brother, though. You hardly know each other."

"I know. Don't you think I thought of that?" Kat's voice rose, her cheeks pink with embarrassment and a hint of annoyance. "I'm half tempted to try talking you into inviting him here so I can see if it will happen again, but that would just

18

be wrong for so many reasons."

The coffee mug hit the table with a bang as Kat took out her frustrations with a jerky motion.

"So I'll assume you are not planning to ask me to get him to drop by?" Gustavia kept her tongue firmly in her cheek.

"Of course I am. That's the problem. I have to know."

This time, Gustavia had no control over the snort. Hearing it, Kat's expression turned mutinous, which did not have the intended effect of quelling Gustavia's gut response. One giggle escaped, then another.

Luckily, laughter is infectious, and before long, Kat started to chuckle. It helped; some of the tension fell away.

CHAPTER FOUR

"Psst."

The hissing noise came from somewhere to her left and sounded slightly muffled, as though whoever was making it had put a hand over their mouth. Something about the voice made her think of Estelle, but why would the spirit bother with an attention-getting bid when all she had to do was speak directly into Kat's mind?

"Who's there?" Kat asked. She cast her mind back over the past few minutes to see if she remembered hearing anything—footsteps, creaking floorboards, the swish of clothing—to indicate the presence of another person entering the room. After a moment, she concluded the sounds were too stealthy. Besides, no one living in the house would sneak up on her—living being the operative word.

"Psst."

There it was again.

"Estelle? Is that you?"

"Not Estelle," came the hissing whisper. Definitely a spirit, or maybe it was Amethyst's angel friend.

"Galmadriel?"

"No." The voice was stronger now.

"I'm sorry, I can't see you, so please, can you give me a hint?" Sensing fear, Kat kept her voice pitched low and gentle.

"Mary Lou."

Kat recognized the name. Mary Lou had been married to Julius; she was Estelle's mother-in-law. Had she been here all this time? Why had she waited so long to make contact?

"Is there something I can do for you? Do you need me to give Julius a message?"

"Why would I need you for that?" Mary Lou clipped her words. "I've got nothing to say to him, but can you tell the girl something for me?"

"You mean Julie? Of course, what is it?" The spirit seemed agitated.

"Tell her to put that light fixture with the star glass back where she found it."

Cryptic words, but Kat promised to relay them and immediately felt Mary Lou's energy settle into a calmer vibrational pattern.

"Thank you. He's coming. He'll help you see what's needed." The whisper faded to a sigh and then to silence before Kat had a chance to ask who was coming, but when she heard footsteps in the hall, she no longer needed to ask. It was Zack; she would recognize his stride anywhere.

Gustavia must have made good on her plan to invite him over. Now that he was here, Kat's mouth went dry, and her stomach dropped toward her toes while what-ifs crowded her thinking.

Instinctively, she turned toward him as he entered the room. He wore jeans and a black sweater that looked impossibly soft as it clung to his torso and stretched tautly across wide shoulders. His hair was gently mussed as though he had run impatient fingers through it time and again. Kat was overwhelmed with the urge to smooth it back into place. To run her hands through those silky, honey-colored strands.

Then it hit her, she could see him. Her vision had cleared again, and it had happened so subtly, so effortlessly she hadn't noticed the change while it was happening. Her heart lurched and began to drum against her ribs; her breath quickened as excitement stole the air from her lungs, clamped down on her chest, and turned her knees to jelly.

Just like before, her body somehow remembered how to see as soon as he came into the room.

How long would it last this time? A minute, an hour? Forever?

Please let it last.

"Sorry, I didn't mean to disturb you." Zack began to turn back toward the door. "Gustavia asked me to visit, but she's in writing mode at the moment. Disturbing her would cost me points."

"No, stay. She'll surface eventually."

Kat sat stock still. She was afraid to move, afraid to lose whatever connection with him had triggered her vision. Nor was she interested in another argument over the veracity of psychic phenomenon. She searched her mind for any other topic and came up with Logan.

"Logan Ellis." The name burst out of her, "Is there any news?" The man had slipped in and out of Oakville as though charmed, wreaking havoc at every turn. Zack continued into the room and slumped down on the couch opposite Kat. He eyed her speculatively.

"Nothing." He spat the word as though it were bitter in his mouth. On a professional front, the man sliding past him at every turn had not been a career-making event. On a personal one, Ellis had kidnapped his sister, and he needed to pay for his actions. Taking Logan's freedom might never feel like enough justice, but it would have to do. "Can't you use your mojo on him? You found that hockey equipment without any trouble; why not Logan?"

Because *the idea scares the bejeesus out of me* didn't seem to be an appropriate answer even if it was the truth. Kat tried to explain.

"You go to a wedding; you hang out with the bride and groom, their friends and family. I go to a wedding; I hang out with all those people *and* the spirits who come along with them. Wherever there's a big group of people, there's always someone repeating the latest gossip. Well, spirits gossip, too."

Zack quirked an eyebrow, then, thinking she could not see him, kept the tone of his voice conversational but allowed a smirk to twist his lips. It took all of Kat's skill to keep from reacting to his deception. So far, he was unaware she could see him. For now, that was the way she wanted it to stay.

"But unlike the living, they can only gossip about what they've actually seen or heard."

"Hearsay and innuendo are not my favorite methods for solving a case." His voice sounded disapproving as he stood up and walked over to take a closer look at the painting of Julius on the mantel. Behind his back, Kat screwed up her face, stuck her tongue out, and made a series of rude hand gestures, but when he turned back around, she was sitting as quietly as before, her face relaxed and eyes staring blankly forward.

"Ju..." Kat trailed off when she remembered that Zack had yet to meet the resident spirits of Hayward House. "...I don't have a direct connection with anyone related to Logan, so I don't have a reliable source for information." Julie's great-grandfather Julius had a tenuous connection with the man, but only because he had worked out a way to track Logan through the vengeful spirit named Billy, who possessed him. Maybe it was time to introduce Zack to their secret weapon, but that wasn't her decision alone. However, if Julius or Estelle were to show up here right now, she would enjoy the spectacle of seeing the ever-arrogant Zack deal with the facts of life after death.

As she looked at him without seeming to look, Kat noticed a difference in her vision from those times when Estelle's presence had allowed her to see—this time, she was less a spectator and more an active participant. Instead of seeing only what Estelle found interesting, Kat could look at anything she chose.

And Kat chose to look at Zack.

Tall and blond like Gustavia—but there the family resemblance ended. Full, kissable lips drew her eye to the shadowy indentation of the cleft in his chin. A strong jaw that appeared chiseled out of stone when he was in an obstinate mood, as he was now, begged to be soothed into a softer line. Then there were those eyes—chocolate brown and warm, but she thought he used them to hide his true feelings more often than not.

Thinking about how attractive he was made Kat feel weird— he looked so much older than the boys she had always admired—then she remembered that the last time she had been visually attracted to someone of the opposite sex, she had been fourteen. It might take her brain a while to catch up.

A little chill crept across Zack's skin. Something was up with Kat, and he hadn't needed his cop sense to figure it out. Was she just distracted, or was she communicating with someone or something he couldn't see?

Nervous mannerisms, tension around the mouth and eyes— she was ready to jump out of her skin. Was it something he said? Knowing she could not see him, looking at her felt oddly voyeuristic, as though he peered at her through a one-way mirror that exposed her every vulnerability. He knew he should look away, but he was riveted.

Peaches and cream skin, a dark swing of hair, eyes the color of cornflowers, and lips of palest pink. He swept his eyes down to take in the contours revealed by the cling of the soft sweater she wore, then farther down, still, to assess a pair of slim, jean-clad legs.

She chewed her nails. Their ragged edges were the only outward sign of stresses he sensed she always took great pains to hide. What was it about those brutally short nails that made him want to cradle her in his arms and smooth that tension away?

Restless energy pulled him back off his seat and over to the window. He hated feeling helpless.

He had given her the once over, and with no idea, she could see him doing it. Kat already thought Zack was arrogant, but this was beyond the pale. Still, once he looked away, her eyes quickly followed the path his had taken.

There was time for a quick glance at the ugly tips of her fingers before she had to pull her eyes back up and focus straight ahead again. Some friends. They could have said something about those hideous nails.

Watching his face during a moment when his guard was down, she saw that her ragged nails stirred something in him, some faint acknowledgment of her vulnerability and a need to protect. It was all there in the way his expression softened, then turned determined. She also saw when he realized there was nothing he could do to help her; the tiny flare of anger he turned toward himself, the frustration that forced him to his feet to pace restlessly to the window.

Not arrogance, then. Just an elevated sense of responsibility for others. Her entire view of him shifted.

An awkward silence fell over them until Gustavia strode into the room a few minutes later to glance first at Zack and then shoot a pointed look at Kat. Kat nodded and shrugged before getting up to leave the room.

Too scared to hope, Kat hoped anyway. Several hours had passed since Zack had left Hayward House, and she could still see. Every time she felt the darkness creeping back, she pulled her mind back to that moment when she had looked at him and forgotten to be blind. That was the moment she realized seeing was effortless but not seeing took work.

Quietly, she called out to Julie's grandmother's spirit. It had been Estelle who made the cryptic prediction that Kat's sight would return. Now it was time to see what further insight the ghost might provide.

She called again and very faintly heard, "On my way."

When Estelle popped into the room, Kat finally got a first look at the spirit who had helped her so much. Petite with salt and pepper hair that waved gently back from a face lined with the kind of wrinkles formed from a lifetime of smiling. Warm, dark eyes with a glint of humor and plenty of compassion shone tearfully from beneath sparse eyebrows inexpertly enhanced with a penciled-in line.

"I'm so happy for you, my dear."

At first, Kat thought the ghost's outline was blurring because Estelle was fading, but then she realized it was the effect of her tears clouding her vision. "I can see you. Oh, Estelle, you're beautiful. Is it real—will it last?"

Estelle nodded, "Forever, now that you've made the right choices," then, too overcome with emotion to speak, she faded out, leaving Kat to come to terms with this new and positive twist.

Gustavia lay sprawled across the chaise lounge, one leg tipped with a bare foot, each toenail painted in brilliant Easter egg colors, was thrown over the chair's arching backrest while the other rested on the floor. Completely absorbed in her work, she tapped away at the wireless keyboard propped up with pillows on her belly.

Too busy to notice before, Kat now noted that Gustavia's attire was very subdued. A batik caftan over striped leggings took the place of her normal uniform—a floaty skirt paired with a brightly colored top. Granted, Kat had only seen her a handful of times and then through the lens of Estelle's perception, but she knew this was a new look for Gustavia.

"How do you write like that? You're practically upside down," Kat observed in a lilting voice. She'd tried for droll but was too excited to pull it off.

How long would it take for Gustavia to catch on?

"Sometimes I need a different perspective to really...," Gustavia froze. Then she tipped her head back and looked at Kat, really looked at her. The keyboard flew, and so did Gustavia—into a backward somersault off the chaise that somehow landed her right in front of Kat. It must have been those impossibly long legs that gave her the reach.

"It worked?" Gustavia searched Kat's eyes, found them clear and shining. "It really worked."

Clutching hands and laughing at nearly the level of a shriek, the two full-grown women hopped in a circle like excited children on Christmas morning, with Gustavia's dog Fritzie running in circles and barking along.

Drawn by the noise, Lola thundered up the stairs, her little stump of a tail wagging so fast the rest of her wiggled along with it. Not far behind Lola, Julie swept into the room to see what the commotion was all about.

"What's going on in here?"

"Kat can see."

"I can see." They spoke together.

Now, three women and two dogs did the insanely happy dance.

Once they had danced themselves out, Gustavia wasted no time. From the top dresser drawer, she grabbed a pair of neon pink socks and pulled them on before jamming her feet onto a pair of short boots.

"Get some shoes on," she nearly shoved Kat out the door, "I'll take you to see your folks. Wow. That word has an entirely new meaning today."

The lump that formed in Kat's throat was large and swift. Leave it to Gustavia to think of exactly the right thing to do. Swallowing through her tears, Kat nodded and left the room to return minutes later, fully shod and carrying a jacket.

"Jules, call Amethyst and start putting together a shopping list. I'll hit the market while Kat visits her folks, and we'll have a celebration dinner."

"No, my parents would love to see you, and then we will both go to the market. No repeats of what happened last time." Kat insisted, fully prepared to forgo the visit rather than put Gustavia in danger.

It was an exhausted Kat who finally returned to her room hours later. The intervening years had been kind to her parents, but she saw changes that wrenched at her heart. Lines of age and a few gray hairs marked the passing time, but their joy washed away many of the traces. Even if everything went black again, Kat had this day to treasure.

The celebration dinner helped her balance out the melancholy mood left over from going home. Good food, a nice Cabernet, and Gustavia, who had dressed for the occasion in the most colorful outfit she could put together. None of it matched, though that was never a concern anyway, you had to give the woman credit for her ability to be festive.

Consequently, it was the wee hours of the morning before Kat stepped into the bathroom to brush her teeth and got the first chance for a long look in the mirror. So many years had fallen into the dark that now, in the light, she felt the reflection portrayed a stranger. Adolescent roundness had given way to leaner planes and angles. Of its own volition, her hand lifted to touch first her cheek, then the mirror itself.

Wide, dark eyes, rosy skin—slightly pale just now—and hair that had deepened at least two shades from the last time she had seen it; she poked her tongue out at the solemn face, then smiled to see remnants of the girl she remembered in the glass.

Don't be stupid, she scolded herself. It's not like you were in a coma or something. Still, the face that peered back at her would take some getting used to.

Teeth brushed, she walked back into the bedroom and climbed under the covers to let sleep finally wash over her. When it did, it brought a series of odd dreams full of sounds and smells but no visuals.

Sometime in the middle of the night, she woke to the softly slurred sound of a whispered voice. It wasn't the first time the night had filled with what sounded like an apology hissing from the darkness.

CHAPTER FIVE

Half an hour after his normal feeding time, Fritzie decided it was time to wake up his person who, he thought, was neglecting her duties. Food he could live without, but he needed to visit his favorite shrub sooner rather than later. Jumping up onto the bed was a no-no. He knew the rules, but maybe if he just stood on his hind feet and rested his front paws on the edge, she wouldn't scold.

Gustavia felt the cold nose as it nudged her awake. She squinted and looked at the clock.

"Sorry, bud. I overslept." The celebration dinner had gone on long into the night. She swung her legs over the side of the bed and reached down to ruffle the little dog's ears. He responded with an ecstatic shimmy and wagged his stumpy tail for all he was worth, then, very pointedly, looked at the door and then back at Gustavia.

She took the hint, pulled on her bathrobe, and moved to the window to pull open the curtains. A light layer of new snow sparkled like millions of tiny diamonds in the morning sun. Frost-coated trees stood like glimmering white sentinels against winter-blue shadow. Gustavia looked out over the fairy landscape and breathed a sigh of appreciation.

Then the sigh caught in her throat as something not bestowed by Mother Nature glinted in the distance. Quickly, she padded on slippered feet into the library, where she knew Tyler kept a pair of field glasses, and in moments, she was back at the window.

At first, she saw nothing out of the ordinary but found what she was looking for on the second pass. Nearly as white as the surrounding snow, a compact car was parked some way down the drive to Hayward House.

With Fritzie and his full bladder forgotten, she raced downstairs to find Julie in the kitchen.

"Get Tyler and go look out my window. There's a car. Someone's watching the house." Gustavia handed the binoculars to Julie with shaking hands. "I'll get Kat and call Zack."

"Kat," an insistent voice hissed in her ear. "Wake up." Kat batted away the hand that shook her shoulder, but it came right back to shake even harder.

"What?" One sleepy eye pried itself open to see Gustavia wearing a neon green chenille bathrobe and carrying a baseball bat. Lit by the sun streaming between the newly opened curtains, the image was beyond vivid.

"We have a situation. Get up."

Senses now on full alert and heart pounding, Kat leaped out of bed and looked around for something to use as a weapon. Though, with her depth perception still off, she couldn't see herself as much of a threat.

Gustavia motioned for Kat to follow her to the suite where she was currently staying.

"Situation?" Kat struggled to slip on a pair of sneakers and walk at the same time, slapped a hand on the wall to stabilize herself when she nearly fell.

"It looks like someone's watching the house. I called Zack; he should be here any minute, but I've heard nothing from Estelle or Julius. Are they around?" Gustavia spoke in a low voice as though someone nefarious might overhear.

Sensing spirit worked as expected about half the time. The best comparison Kat could name was that it operated similarly to those real estate radio signs. Yeah, you could pick up the vibe, but you had to be tuned to the right frequency and within a radius of the transmitter. The difference was that those signs are always fixed in place while spirits move around a lot, so it was like hitting a moving target.

And sometimes they didn't want to talk.

This was one of those times. When Kat's searching energy field touched Estelle's, it was gently rebuffed. She got only a split second to assess the ghost's frame of mind.

"They're outside, but they don't seem worried at all. I could swear Estelle just giggled at me."

Gustavia sighed and relaxed for the first time since she spotted the car. She trusted Estelle.

If Zack was on his way to the house, Kat had no intention of greeting him in her jammies, so she suggested to Gustavia that they would both be better prepared for what might happen if they were dressed for the day.

Back in her room, she chose a soft sweater, her fingers automatically checking for the button that marked it as blue before she remembered she no longer needed that particular accessibility option. She hardly had time to tie her shoes before the doorbell bonged. Kat met Gustavia on the stairs, and together they hurried toward the front door just in time to see Julie pull it open.

Zack stood on the porch; the serious expression on his face

might have carried more weight if not for the smile twitching around his lips and the twinkle in his eye. Beside him stood a pair of teenage girls who barely looked old enough to drive.

The taller of the two, all knees and elbows, wore a pair of leggings—her concession to the cold weather—under a multi-tiered batik skirt in shades ranging from moss to lime green. The skirt was paired with a predominantly orange tie-dyed tee and topped with a puffy winter coat. Half a dozen beaded necklaces completed the ensemble, and her mouse-brown hair was inexpertly braided to mimic one of Gustavia's more elaborate styles. She stood next to Zack, shoulders rounded, head down in shame.

The other, shorter by about six inches, was dressed similarly in a blue patterned skirt with several scarves tied around the waist and topped with a rainbow-striped sweater. She attempted a defiant stance, one she might have pulled off if her fear-widened eyes hadn't given her away.

Trying to sound stern, Zack spoke directly to his sister, "It seems you have a couple of stalkers."

"Not stalkers," the shorter girl corrected, her frightened eyes moving frantically between Zack and Gustavia, "fans. Gustavia's biggest fans. We weren't stalking anyone," her voice shook, "we just wanted to see if we could meet her." She pointed to Gustavia.

Kat heard a masculine snort from somewhere behind her and had to work hard to keep a straight face. From the corner of her eye, she saw Gustavia fighting a smile of her own.

Gustavia stepped forward, intending to gently address the red-faced girl who had not yet spoken. She had to lean down to make eye contact. "What's your name?"

"Beth. I'm Beth. I'm sorry, we didn't mean any harm...it's just that we...we had these books, you know? We thought you might sign them. We didn't think we were doing anything

33

wrong. There's a museum here, so we thought it was okay, you know? Like, it wasn't trespassing if it was a public place. My parents will kill me if I get arrested." Tears leaked down her cheeks then she turned on her friend to say hotly, "You told me we wouldn't get into trouble. You promised and now look. I'll be grounded until I'm forty."

Looking at Zack, Kat saw his lips twitch again before he managed to school his face back into stern lines. Catching his eye, she gave him a warning look. The girls were frightened enough without him making it worse.

"No one is getting arrested," he returned her look with a steady gaze, then turned to the second girl and asked her name.

"Meg Wolcott." Her bravado fading, Meg considered Gustavia. "We didn't expect you to call the PoPo. We only came here to get your autograph and maybe talk to you for a few minutes." She looked away and mumbled, "It's not a federal offense."

A second snort escaped before Tyler could hold it back. Julie poked an elbow into his ribs, but it was only for show. She was shaking so hard with held-back laughter that she couldn't put any force behind the attempt.

Zack stepped around the two girls, gave his sister a one-armed hug, and said, "I'll leave these two hardened criminals in your capable hands, Sis. Call me if you need the cuffs." With a last grin at the others, he walked out the door.

"Sis?" Meg looked at Gustavia, "He's your brother?"

Before Gustavia could answer, Beth dramatically slapped a hand to her forehead and pinned her friend with a glare. "You called him the PoPo. Right in front of her." Now it was Meg's turn to hang her head in shame.

That was when Tyler lost it. Julie had to drag him, still howling, out of the room.

Beth's face burned with embarrassment as she said quietly to

Gustavia, "I'm sorry. We'll go now." She grabbed Meg's arm and turned toward the door.

"No, wait." Fritzie nudged past Gustavia to stand by the door. The frantic way he looked at her and then at the door said time was of the essence, and she had made him wait long enough. When the door opened, Julie's dog Lola, a large but mostly friendly boxer, bounced out from wherever she had been hiding to join Fritzie in a mad dash for the bushes.

While she waited for the two dogs to finish doing their morning sniffing tour around the yard, Gustavia chatted easily with her two visitors. Before Fritzie pranced back across the porch, Beth and Meg were happily talking about the path that had led them to Hayward House.

Kat busied herself with pulling out breakfast ingredients while listening to Beth talk about the mythological themes present in Gustavia's latest books.

"...said we had drawn a sophisticated parallel between Ember's search for his mother and Campbell's monomyth, the hero's journey."

Meg took up the story, "We did a collage and a huge presentation where we also compared Ember to Jason Bourne. It was awesome."

By the time the two teens left Hayward House, they had enough information to do a paper on Gustavia herself, and Kat had come to a decision. It was time to go home. Moving in with Julie and Tyler had seemed sensible after Logan kidnapped Gustavia. Until now, Kat had gone along with the plan, but with her visual impairment no longer a factor, she needed to be in her own space. She didn't think Logan would target her, nor did Julius when she asked him privately.

"I have close neighbors, a security system, and beings of spirit to watch over me. I'll be fine," she explained that night

35

over dinner when Tyler argued that she would be safest by staying put, but Kat refused to be swayed. After dinner, she went back to her rooms to begin packing her things.

Gustavia and Julie followed, ostensibly to help but mostly to continue trying to talk her out of leaving.

"I appreciate everything you've said. I do. But I'm in no more danger there than I am here. Probably a lot less if we're being honest since Logan and Billy barely knows I exist."

Kat knew Gustavia would have moved out after the wedding if Finn hadn't talked her into adding that half bath at her place. It was supposed to be a minor remodeling job, but he'd managed to keep her place in a state of chaos for weeks—he had no intention of letting her go home alone.

"Take Lola with you," Julie suggested. Lola came across as mostly sweet—even slightly goofy—but the one time Logan had tried to break into Hayward House, she proved she could handle herself while chasing off a bad guy. The dog had a soft spot for Kat.

"No. Thank you, but no. I love her to bits, but my yard is just too small. It's why I never wanted a service dog."

The sense that her life was about to begin again filled Kat with purpose.

CHAPTER SIX

After a couple of minutes spent fumbling with the key, Kat finally closed her eyes and unlocked the door by feel. Undoubtedly, having her vision back would make most things in her life easier, but in the meantime, she would have to adjust.

From the outside, the house looked as she remembered from childhood visits—right down to the Madame Zephyr sign beside the door.

Eyes still tightly shut, she dropped her bags just inside the door and closed it behind her. More used to moving through the space in darkness, she hung up her coat before making her way toward the back of the house.

Everything felt familiar. She breathed in the powdery scent of the dried flower arrangement on the hall table, the polish her mother used on the dining room table—a task she would be handling from here on out—the sound of the old, wide-plank floorboards in the hallway leading to the kitchen.

Home.

Would the kitchen look the same? It had been long years

since she sat, warm in a pool of sunlight, at her grandmother's honey-colored pine table and counted the teapots lined up on the shelf by the door.

Four shelves, four pots on each shelf, meant there were sixteen in total. Kat's eyes tracked to her favorite, a vintage porcelain confection painted in a stylized pattern of flowers. It featured stacking creamer and sugar bowls and still held the things her grandmother had stored inside. Little handwritten notes, addresses for people long dead, a marble, several heart-shaped stones, recipes, half a dozen used twist ties, some rubber bands, a small key, and three packets of dried yeast that had to be decades past their expiration date by now. Nothing of vital importance, but sorting through those things and touching them brought back memories of a simpler childhood. The time before spirit came into her life.

Kat opened her eyes and blinked at the darkness, only a shade or two lighter than the back of her eyelids. At first, she thought her vision was going again, and her heart skipped a beat, then began to thump in her chest. After a moment of panic, she realized she had forgotten to switch on the light.

More new habits, she sighed and made a mental note to remember for next time. During the brief periods when channeling Estelle had given back her sight, Kat had been far too busy dealing with the new sensations to spend extra time looking around.

Now, she wandered from room to room and memory to memory. Torn between older, more visual memories and newer ones that only carried touch, scent, and sound—seeing each room as it was now, she felt both at home and, at the same time, like a stranger seeing everything anew.

Kat dragged a finger through the light layer of dust that testified to the fact no one had been in the house for weeks and weeks. With a sense of purpose, she spent the next couple of hours exploring every nook and cranny, dusting as she went and making a mental list of things to purchase. Light bulbs made the list for the first time in her adult life.

Finally feeling more settled, more connected, a tired Kat carried her bags upstairs to unpack.

Twenty-four hours.

That was the brief respite before the first phone call came in.

"Hello?" Kat's talking caller ID announced a number she had never heard before.

"Hello, is this Kathleen?"

"Kat," she corrected automatically.

"This is Paul," he said his name as though he expected her to know who he was already.

"Paul," she repeated his name in bewilderment.

"I assume your mom didn't tell you I'd be calling."

"No, she didn't." Just like that, Kat knew the matchmaking had begun. "Let me guess, she ran into you in the grocery store and started asking subtle questions to see if you were single," Kat predicted.

"She and my mom are in some kind of knitting club together."

"Ah, so they're in cahoots."

"Yes, I believe they've formed a gang that goes around forcing susceptible men into making embarrassing phone calls to unsuspecting women. The key word there is unsuspecting." His droll tone made her smile.

"Who's the ringleader? Your mom or mine?"

"Oh, I think it's a joint position. So what do you think? Take a chance on a date with me? I mean, we've both been duped. We already know we have that in common."

Kat thought about it for a moment. She trusted her mother's taste, so how bad could it be?

"Sure, why not."

Five minutes into dinner, Kat knew this first date would also be a last date. Paul was nice enough and had a wonderful sense of humor, but the extra family members who tagged along made it difficult for her to take him seriously. Standing right behind his left shoulder, Aunt Gertrude kept up a running list of his many positive attributes. She wore one of those zip-front housedresses in vivid shades of magenta and sky blue. That, coupled with how she waved her arms around, made it incredibly difficult for Kat to focus on the earnest and humble Paul, who would have been mortified to hear his aunt's words. The woman should have had a career in infomercials. Before the appetizers hit the table, Kat knew more about Paul than he did about himself, including how incredibly early he had mastered the art of potty training.

Too. Much. Information.

The others—a third cousin, a grandfather, and two uncles just wanted her to assure their families they were happy in the afterlife—and a little yellow ball of fur circled the group, yipping incessantly.

At least dealing with his spirit entourage had given her something to concentrate on besides the nervous flutter just under her breastbone.

Kat pressed finger and thumb to the bridge of her nose, hoping to stave off the headache that threatened to rage into full throb. It had been easier to tune spirit out when she only had to deal with one of her senses. Now that she could see them, it was harder to ignore their voices.

"...the London office." She pulled her attention back to the conversation. With no idea what Paul had been talking about, she nodded and hoped her response was appropriate.

When Gertrude mentioned how his "tushy" looked when he

was a baby, Kat choked on her drink and abruptly excused herself to the ladies' room, surreptitiously motioning for Gertrude to follow her. Once in relative privacy, she rounded on the spirit.

"Stop! You have to stop." She softened her voice, "Look, I can tell that you care about him and want him to be happy, but you have to know he wouldn't appreciate you telling me all the intimate details of his life. Give us some privacy and take the rest of the family with you."

"I'm sorry," Gertrude said. "He's such a nice boy. Please give him another chance."

Kat grinned. "Get that dog away from me, and you've got a deal."

She returned to the table, determined to enjoy the rest of her dinner.

Paul looked up as she approached the table, a pleasant smile on his face. He was attractive enough, she supposed. Crisply curling dark hair and even white teeth flashed above a square chin. Maybe his top lip was a little thin, but he was the kind of cute any woman would give a second look.

"I'm sorry," he said as soon as she sat down, "I've been rambling on about my job this whole time when I'd much rather learn more about you. Tell me, what do you do?"

And there it was—the dreaded question. Kat searched his face looking for some clue that would give her an idea of how he might react. This was an unexpected aspect of dating. Since she had already decided against a second date—even if Gertrude toned it down a notch, this guy had way too much baggage in the spirit department—Kat took a deep breath and brazened it out.

"I'm a psychic medium."

Paul's eyebrows shot toward his hairline, and suddenly the look on his face was no longer cute.

"What did you say?"

Stomach now dropping toward her shoes, Kat maintained an even tone, "I said I am a psychic medium," then she pinned him with a look that just dared him to make a big deal of it. Would he turn out to be a skeptic or use this chance to try and finagle a reading out of her?

Instead, he swallowed heavily and changed the subject. Given a choice between finding his attitude mortifying or amusing, Kat chose the latter.

She even managed to keep her smirk on the inside when she caught him surreptitiously glancing at his watch while she was checking the clock on the wall behind him. Would this disaster of a date ever end?

Clearly, this dating thing would be much more complicated than she had expected. Kat drank a private toast to hoping the next one would be less awkward while she listened to his nervous attempt to ignore the elephant in the room—not too easy when said elephant was twirling a flaming baton and dancing while wearing a hot pink tutu.

When he dropped her back at Hayward House, his feet barely touched the porch before he hot-footed it back to his car. Kat waggled her fingers at his taillights as they disappeared from view.

The next time she and her friends got together to dish about their experiences, she finally had a story to tell. That alone made the entire evening worthwhile. Kat threw her head back, laughed out loud, and walked out the door.

CHAPTER SEVEN

Fifteen steps from the bathroom door to the corner where she kept her fitness equipment. Kat counted each step as she walked, even though it was a habit she no longer needed. Half an hour on the treadmill—or dreadmill—as she preferred to call it, was on her list for the morning. She had just settled into her running stride when the doorbell pealed twice, followed by frantic knocking on her front door.

"Give me a minute," she muttered while the knocking and ringing continued. Kat felt for the braille label pasted over the on/off switch and paced herself as the belt slowed to a stop. How long, she wondered, would it take before she got used to looking for the switch with her eyes instead of using her fingertips?

"Who is it?" She called out before she remembered she could have just looked through the peephole. So many changes. A little frisson of nervous energy settled in her belly. Spontaneous visitors were not a rarity in her line of business, but this wasn't business, she knew, when her senses went on alert anyway.

"Kat, it's Zack. I need your help. Please, open the door. Hurry."

Since her depth perception was still a work in progress, Kat slammed her hip on the hall table as she made her way to the door. She winced as the sharp point bruised her tender flesh. Stumbling and dashing away tears of pain, she pulled open the door to let him in. "What is it? What happened? Is it…"

"No, sorry." He should have realized her mind would go there first. "No, it's nothing to do with Logan. Everyone is safe. Everyone except a little boy named Noel, who went missing from his house over in Landon this morning. His mother is frantic." Zack reached into his jacket pocket, pulled out a photo and a small stuffed dog. He handed her the picture, which she looked at briefly before passing it back.

He then pressed the stuffed toy into her hand and ignored the little spark of awareness that rose up in his belly. Something about her always triggered that same intensity as his cop sense, a recognition that stabbed into his gut and twisted.

"You want me to help you find him? I thought you didn't believe in me."

"You're not exactly Santa Claus, and I'm not even sure why I came here, but I thought you might be able to help. Maybe I was wrong." He reached for the toy she still held, intending to pull it away from her. As he stepped near, her breath caught.

He trusted her enough to come here when he could be out searching for the boy. There was hope for him yet.

"No, I want to try." She yanked the toy back, ignoring the electric feeling of his hand brushing against hers, and after a short tugging match where she felt the toy starting to rip, he finally let go and raised his hands in surrender.

"It's a little boy. Of course, I'll do what I can." She reached out and laid a hand on his arm. "Tell me about him. How did it happen?"

"He's four. He was wearing a red striped shirt, blue pants, and snow boots. He's blond, blue eyes..." he trailed off when she held up her hand.

"None of that visual stuff helps me. What I need is a sense of his family life. What was happening right before he went missing?"

"Mom was doing laundry while the boy played in his room. Dad was at work. He does maintenance for the apartment complex down on Grove Street. His boss sent him to the city to pick up pipes and a gas fitting. If it was a kidnapping, we've ruled out the father, and he's on his way home now. No friction there. Happy family. The front door was open. No signs of forced entry or a struggle. No known enemies."

Kat clutched the stuffed dog and tried to concentrate on little Noel to pick up the sensory cues that would lead to finding the boy while Zack paced. His energy was like a caged beast pushing at the bars, trying to break free from confinement.

Distracting.

"I need quiet. Your energy is frantic." Kat explained. He huffed out a breath.

"This is time sensitive. Can you do whatever it is you did with the hockey equipment or not?"

"Yes—no. Maybe. Just give me five minutes of peace. Go into the kitchen, down the hall to your right, brew a pot of coffee, and let me think."

"Where's the...."

"Zack. Please, go figure it out. Quietly." She handed back the stuffed dog; there was nothing more it could tell her.

With a shrug of acceptance, he turned, his booted feet sounding unnaturally loud on the hardwood floor, and practically stomped his way down the hallway toward the kitchen. Kat shook her head at his retreating back and moved toward the dining room where she normally met with clients.

45

Thoughts of him poking through her cupboards crowded out her ability to concentrate on the little boy who might be in trouble. What she needed was a distraction from his presence in her home so she could concentrate.

To give her hands something to do, Kat reached into the well-polished antique cabinet, pulled out a small bag of rune stones, and dumped them onto the table. Just touching them helped ground the energy flowing through her and let her begin to focus on something other than the voice in the back of her head. The one that kept repeating, *there's a man in your kitchen. He's touching your stuff.*

Kat's eyes lost focus as she ran her nimble fingers through the runes. After a short time, she began sorting through the stones, picking up first one, then another, turning them over with her fingers and clearing the channels that spirit generally used to send their messages.

"Zack, does the boy have any family on the other side? Grandparents, aunts, uncles?"

"Grandmother, on his father's side. Her name was June Hamilton," he called back. She heard him opening cabinets and drawers.

"Oh, I knew her. Noel is Will's boy? Will was a year ahead of me in school; he married a girl named Sandy. No, Sonjia. Something like that."

"You going to climb every branch on their family tree, or are you going to help me find that boy?" Zack walked back into the room, and Kat could see the tension coming off him in waves.

"Do I tell you how to do your job? No. Now back off and let me do mine."

Once he'd returned to the kitchen, Kat heard the furnace kick on, the blower sounding unnaturally loud. When it shut off, the silence sounded even louder until she heard the bubbling gurgle of the coffee maker.

"I'm not getting anything." She smelled the coffee now. Rich and dark and seductive. It made her feel warm and protected; it smelled like home, like comfort, like safety.

Zack called out from the kitchen. "I can't find the filters."

"Wait, you haven't made coffee yet?"

"I can't find the filters." He repeated, exaggerating each word as though he thought her stupid. "Waste of time anyway. Anything could be happening to that boy by now."

"No. Nothing bad has happened. He's safe." She would address his tactlessness later, "Noel—he can smell coffee." Kat rose to pace the room. "He's someplace warm, comfortable." Now that she had the sense of him, it was easy to pick out the threads, tell which sensations had been his and which had been her own. The loud furnace noise meant a basement, maybe? Some kind of closet?

"Call your guys, tell them he is in a small space near a furnace, and he can smell coffee brewing. Wherever he is, he feels safe because he has been there before. It feels familiar to him.

When Zack just stood there, she walked over and gave him a shove. "What are you waiting for? Call them." Instead, he started to pull her toward the door.

"Grab a jacket. Don't you want to see for yourself? It's a five-minute drive with the lights on." Thinking of a mother frantic to find her child, Kat quickly pulled a coat from the closet and followed him outside, putting her excitement down to helping a lost boy and not the sizzle of his hand touching her arm.

Sun sparkling off the patches of remaining snow blasted light at eyes still unused to such brightness, and Kat put a hand to her forehead for shade. Zack concentrated on his driving but still managed to keep her in his peripheral vision.

"There's a pair in the glove box."

"What?" His words confused her.

"Sunglasses," he reached across, pressed the button to open the cubby, and handed her his aviators. They would be huge on her small face, but at least her eyes would be protected.

Grateful for how they cut the glare, she never thought about how she looked. Too many years of not seeing herself in mirrors made it all too easy to forget about appearances. She would have been shocked to know Zack thought she looked adorable in his sunglasses.

It seemed they had barely pulled out of her driveway before they were turning into a small housing development. Kat remembered passing through here with her grandfather when she was younger. To see an area that had once been a large field now populated with a series of houses built from a similar pattern messed with her sense of place. It felt like she had traveled through time.

The third house on the left, the one with flashing lights and cruisers parked in front was the one Zack made a beeline for, leaving Kat to follow more slowly. Before she reached the front steps, a whisper sounded in her ear.

"Over here." It was faint, little more than a hiss. Kat lagged even farther behind and looked around to see where the noise was coming from. Down the narrow path between the two houses, the ground was already bare of snow but still felt frozen under her feet. Kat followed the voice until she heard, "look, there."

Unless you were looking for it, you might not notice the basement window was ajar or that there was a small smear of mud on the sill.

Relief washed over Kat, some of it hers, some coming from the presence that had guided her to this place. The one she now realized had been feeding her information all along.

Leaning down, she nudged the window gently to see if a small boy could fit through the opening. When it swung wide on hinges mounted to the top, she knew this was the place. Little Noel could have easily pushed the window open and slid inside. Lifting Zack's sunglasses off her nose, Kat peered in but could not see the boy anywhere. She straightened and hurried back to where Zack was standing on the porch with two women.

Both women were visibly distraught, one more than the other, her shoulders rounded, arms folded at her waist. There was a fragility about her as she tried to hold herself together— Noel's mother, that tore at Kat's heartstrings. As Kat mounted the steps, Sonjia reached up to run a shaky hand through her already mussed hair. It was obviously not the first time she had performed the action that day. Tears dripped from her shadow-smudged eyes to make tracks down her pale face.

"We'll find him," Zack was saying. "We are following every possible lead." He didn't want to admit how he had gotten one of those leads or that he was banking on Kat's being right.

He turned when he heard her feet crossing the porch, and she beckoned him to follow her. There was no reason to get Sonjia's hopes up, though Kat was positive Noel was curled up and sleeping in that basement. She led Zack to the window and showed him what she had found.

He wasted no time making his way back to where Sonjia stood. "Did you find something?" Hope made her voice rise.

"Who lives next door?" Zack asked.

The other woman spoke, "I'm Melinda, that's my house, but I'd have heard Noel if he came in. I was making coffee when I heard Sonjia screaming outside. The front door is right next to my kitchen."

Kat felt a surge of emotion. Coffee.

"Not if he went in through the basement window," she

pointed out.

"Those windows should all be latched...." Melinda's eyes narrowed, "unless my husband has been sneaking smokes down there, he promised to quit." Melinda was already headed down the steps, Sonjia hard on her heels.

"I'll kill him if that little boy has hurt himself."

"I'll hug him if we find Noel safe and sound. Then I'll help you kill him."

Kat followed Zack, who followed Sonjia into Melinda's house. Four pairs of feet clattered down the wooden basement stairs as Sonjia called out, "Noel, are you down here?"

No answer.

Maybe Kat had been mistaken, but she didn't think so. At that moment, the furnace kicked on, and, looking toward the noise, she saw a small space under a set of shelves. From out of the shadowy space poked a small, snow-booted foot.

"Look, there," she pointed. Zack beat Sonjia by half a hair's breadth and, pulling a small flashlight from his belt, hunkered down to direct the beam into the space. Tired from his adventure, Noel was curled up on a pile of rags, sound asleep. Clutched tightly in his arms, a bedraggled cat blinked in the sudden light and began to purr.

With a huge grin on his face, Zack stood, then turned to Sonjia, "He's fine. Look for yourself," and handed her the light. Seeing Noel safe, his mother sank to her knees, sobs of relief shaking her shoulders as her son slept on.

"I'm so sorry. My house was the one place we didn't bother to check because I was so sure there was no way he could have gotten past me," Melinda's voice wobbled. She was on the edge of sobbing, half from relief and half from blaming herself.

"I'm betting he followed that cat through the window. He's been watching it for the past few days and worrying over whether 'poor kitty' was cold or hungry."

The two women comforted each other as soft snores and purrs emanated from under the shelf. If that cat didn't go home with Noel, Kat would eat her shoe.

Still grinning, Zack called off the Amber Alert and personally assured Will Hamilton his son was safe before leaving the two women to deal with the child and cat. There was a spring in his step as he escorted Kat back up the stairs. This part of the job made it all worthwhile—the times when it went right when no one got hurt.

Protect and serve. Words to live by.

Now that it was all over, Kat felt lightheaded, breathless. It was the adrenaline rush. It could not be Zack's hand on the small of her back as he guided her toward the car. A quick look at the clock on his dash said the whole thing had taken about an hour, but it felt like only a few minutes had passed.

"How often do you get to help people like this?" No wonder he had chosen this line of work.

"Most days are less dramatic; routine traffic stops, breaking up bar fights, the occasional domestic call. During tourist season, there's a lot of D&D—drunk and disorderly—shoplifting is a problem during the summer months. Last year I had to talk a naked man down off the flagpole at the marina."

"I'll assume he had a good reason for being up there."

"Climbing the flagpole he did on a dare. The naked part...well..." Zack shrugged.

"Better not to know, I think. Why here? What made you leave the city?"

Some of the easiness of the past few minutes dropped away, and while he didn't exactly avoid the question, Kat had the impression that his answer was a half-truth at best.

"Lateral move and the chance to reconnect with my sister."

Maybe he would tell her the rest someday, but for now, she

accepted his answer and changed the subject.

"I've got to get one of these." Kat glanced around the interior of the cruiser.

"A cop car? You planning to join the force?"

With rolling eyes, "No, silly. A car. I'm tired of having to be carted around everywhere I want to go. Guess I should learn how to drive first, though."

"You don't know how?" Of course, she didn't. What a dumb question. "I could teach you if you like. I'm off tomorrow."

"You're not one of those teachers who freaks out at every little thing, are you?"

"No idea. Pick you up around 10 am?" He pulled up in front of her place.

"It's a date," Kat did a mental facepalm, "I didn't mean…."

His look turned intense, "Thank you for everything you did today."

She waved his thanks away. "See you tomorrow." Kat got out of the car before another stupid comment could fall out of her mouth.

After he pulled away, he thought about her for a long time.

"While my friends were learning to drive, I was learning to navigate through a world of darkness. Braille, counting steps, tagging my clothes to keep from looking like a freak, learning how to cook, how to organize my kitchen, money origami."

"Money origami? That's a bar trick, right?"

"Maybe for the sighted, but for me, I had to learn different ways of folding my money so I could tell the bills apart. You'd be surprised how many cashiers take advantage of the blind."

He had seen worse things happen to people, but her quiet admission still sparked a seething mass of unexpected emotion in him. He wanted nothing more than to go back in time and protect her. Her next comment surprised him even more.

"I was lucky, though. My parents were determined that I learn to be as independent as possible. They couldn't afford to send me to a special school, so my mom put her research skills to work and learned how to teach me all of those things herself. She was relentless. She even learned Braille. There were times I hated her for pushing me so hard."

"It must have been difficult for her, too."

Kat nodded. "She worried, even after practically pushing me out of the house when my grandmother passed and left me this place, but she always encouraged me to test the limits of what I could accomplish." Tears welled up in her eyes but did not spill over.

"How did she feel about...?" As soon as the words left his lips, he wished he had not brought the subject up.

"About me being a medium? You can say the word, Zack. I'm not ashamed of what I do. Not anymore." It was nothing less than the truth. "It may not have been my dream job, but I've been able to help people find peace with some terrible losses. What I do is rewarding on many levels. Helping you find that boy yesterday was unforgettable."

Changing the subject, Zack said, "I think it's time you made up for some of those lost experiences. Let's go teach you how to drive."

"You know, I'm nervous all of a sudden."

"Come on. You'll be fine."

"But I don't even have a learner's permit. I'd be breaking the law."

Zack laughed at that. "I think you'll be safe from prosecution. Grab a jacket. It's cold outside."

Now that second thoughts had descended, Kat started casting around for anything that might get her out of the situation. But, coming up with nothing, she resigned herself to Zack's teaching her to drive. She fully expected him to be impatient and abrupt. Dread settled over her as she pulled on a jacket and followed him out the door.

Zack drove them to the municipal parking lot, empty on a Sunday at this time of day. As he did, he kept up a running description of what he was doing while he drove and what he wanted her to do when they got there. For this first foray, he only wanted her to get used to the feel of the pedals and steering.

As he explained how the gas and brake pedals worked and what each gear was used for, she felt a pleasant sense of anticipation welling up inside. This adventure might just turn out to be fun. She asked questions, and his patient answers helped release the tension she felt in his presence. The man ran hot and cold.

When he laughed at her rapid-fire grilling over the finer points of where to position her hands on the steering wheel, she became distracted by the crinkles in the corner of his eyes, by the deep tones in his voice. They sent shivers through her until she had trouble focusing on what he wanted her to do.

Oh well, she was a quick study, and if a sixteen-year-old could learn how to drive, there was no reason she should find it any more difficult.

Zack stopped the car, and before she knew it, Kat was behind the wheel. He helped her adjust the seat and then directed her to set the mirrors.

"Now, firmly press on the brake and move the shifter from park to drive. Then, release the brake and apply gentle pressure to the gas pedal."

Gentle pressure is a relative term, Kat realized, as she thought she was barely touching the pedal, but the car shot forward. She mashed the brake and then held on tight as they lurched to a stop. Breathing deeply to quiet her nerves, she gave Zack a sidelong glance expecting him to be annoyed.

Instead, to her surprise, he had a mile-wide grin on his face.

"Sorry," Kat's face flamed red.

"You did fine. Now, try it again. Just ease into it."

This time she knew what to expect, so the takeoff was smoother, more controlled, and she was fine until she got to the end of the lot and overshot the turn a bit, and had to slam on the brakes again.

Still smiling, Zack put her at ease, showed her how to correct the error before directing her to continue driving.

After the fourth circle around the perimeter, Kat began having fun. This wasn't so bad after all. Zack's reassuring presence increased her confidence. The man was a natural-born instructor with a surprising amount of patience.

Six times around, then seven, and Kat was becoming bored. The car rolled to a stop. She looked over at Zack.

"Now what?" This must have been what it was like to be sixteen and just learning to drive, that feeling of anticipation tinged with fear. Added to the nerve-tightening effect of being nearly shoulder-to-shoulder with a man who smelled like sin, Kat savored the delicious shot of adrenaline. It made her feel reckless.

"Am I ready for the road?"

"Let's try turning left first." The quirk of his eyebrow was at odds with the twinkle in his eye. He was enjoying this, she could tell. She felt daring around him for the first time ever and was tempted to flirt. Though, just as the thought crossed her mind, so did the realization that the last time she had done any flirting was when she was fourteen. Never mind.

Instead, she scoffed. "Come on, give me a real challenge."

The twinkle in his eye turned wicked. "Okay then. How about a few circles in reverse."

Kat dropped the shifter into place and turned to look over her right shoulder. Without thinking, she put her foot down on the gas pedal with the same pressure she had used to go forward. The car lurched and, when she turned the wheel, went in the opposite direction to the one she had intended. A soft "Oh," of surprise was all she had time for as she cranked the wheel hard in the other direction, overcompensating, and the car lurched again, then swayed as she turned the wheel the other way.

Breathing hard, she jammed the brake and slammed the shifter into park while the car was still rocking. When she heard a muffled snort from her passenger, Kat spoke between clenched teeth, "You did that on purpose. Why didn't you warn me the steering was different?"

"You asked for a challenge." He wasn't even trying to hide the amusement now, and when she glared at him, he only laughed harder.

"I fail to see the humor." But seeing him more relaxed and open than she ever had before did something to her. Zack's laugh was infectious, and she found herself laughing with him. As much as she wanted to stay mad, seeing him cut loose a little showed her a different side of him.

Between his job, the drama with his family, and the worry she could always see hovering over him with Logan still gunning for Gustavia, the man had a lot on his plate. If getting tickled over her aborted attempt to back up helped him release some tension, she could live with that.

"You want to try again?"

Providing him with a little comic relief was fine, but her pride would not allow her to quit. "Of course."

This time, she was prepared and, with some effort, managed a complete circle, then showed off a second one in the other direction before stopping to swap places with him so he could take her home.

CHAPTER EIGHT

Julie called a few hours later with an invite for a girl's night at Hayward House. Kat knew from her inflection that Julie had something to share.

Amethyst picked Kat up on her way.

"Hey, you changed your hair," Kat noticed right away. Amethyst's chin-length, blunt-cut wedge of hair, tinted with a pale lavender hue for the past year and a half, was now a brighter, more vibrant color.

"I thought it was time for something different."

"I love it. It looks like…" Kat paused to dredge up a long-forgotten memory, "cotton candy."

"Not entirely what I was going for." Amethyst's deep voice always seemed at odds with her tiny frame. "Julie seemed excited. I feel a bet coming on. Ten on what's got her going?"

"Always." Kat had already run through the various options. Logic told her wedding photos were the safest bet.

"She's pregnant."

"Wedding photos."

Kat thought Amethyst seemed quieter than usual during most

of the drive to Julie's and was surprised when she pulled over and turned in her seat with a searching look.

"Your aura is all twingly."

"Is that bad or good?" Kat wondered since it was obviously a made-up word.

"Can I…" without waiting for an answer, Amethyst thrust her hand toward Kat and began plucking at whatever it was that she alone could see.

"What are you…?"

"Shh, let me do this."

Kat subsided and let Amethyst poke, pick and prod her aura, then smooth it with her hand.

"That's better," Kat felt no different until the car started to move again. Whatever debris had been twingling up her aura must have been connected to the dimensional aspect of her vision because Ammie had just corrected that pesky depth perception problem.

"Hurry up. We've been waiting for you." Julie called out from somewhere inside when Gustavia swung open the door. Amethyst tossed their coats on an empty chair and asked, "What's the big news?"

"I picked up the wedding pictures this morning."

Amethyst groaned and passed over Kat's winnings.

With great anticipation, Julie pulled the box out and started leafing through the pages of the photo albums inside. They could have looked at the images on her computer since a disk of the photos was also part of her package, but this way seemed more ceremonial.

As a wedding gift, the gallery owner where Julie showed her work had gotten another up-and-coming art photographer to shoot the wedding. His name was Johann, and since Julie had opted for him to do primarily candid shots, he had remained as unobtrusive as possible and still managed to capture the entire night with shot after exquisite shot.

For the next half hour, there was nothing but a chorus of oohs, ahs, giggles, and sniffles as they relived the day through the images in the book. Then Julie turned over the last page, and Kat nearly choked as the color drained from her face.

Somehow—impossibly—Johann had captured the exact moment her eyes had locked onto Zack's. It was all there, in living color, the look on his face almost a sneer, her eyes clear and snapping at his tone.

And off to one side, nearly in shadow and slightly fuzzy in the shallow depth of field the photographer had used, a face she could swear belonged to her own grandmother.

All Kat could think was that it was a good thing she was sitting down because knees made from Jell-0 might not hold her. She pointed a trembling finger at the image and tried to speak, but her mouth was too dry.

Gustavia looked over at Kat and saw nothing but huge eyes in a shocked white face. "Kat, are you all right? What's wrong?"

Though she opened her mouth, words just wouldn't come.

"Here, drink this." Gustavia pressed her glass of water into Kat's hand, helped guide it to her lips.

"What happened?" For the second time that day, Amethyst busied herself flicking bits of dark, fear-stained light from Kat's aura.

"Julie, do you know who this is? Right here." She pointed to the partially visible face. Maybe it was just someone who looked like her grandmother. One of Tyler's aunts. She'd been too caught up to look at every guest.

"I don't recognize her. Let me get Tyler." With a concerned glance back at Kat, Julie hurried from the room to return with her husband in tow.

"Doesn't look familiar, but it's hard to tell. If the photo was just a bit lighter or clearer."

"Oh, I can fix that." Julie grabbed the pack of image disks from the box and left the room.

More composed now, Kat followed the others to the studio, where they all watched as Julie booted up her computer and opened up an image manipulation program.

After a few minutes of fussing with the controls, she had the shadowy face about as bright and clear as it would get. At Kat's intake of breath, Julie turned toward her.

"It's her. The original Madame Zephyr."

Before she could help herself, the words burst out of Julie's mouth, "Well, now you know how that feels."

Shocked stares prompted Julie to apologize, which netted her a snort from Kat. "Had that coming, didn't I? I'm not sure why I was so surprised to see her there. I guess I wasn't expecting it is all."

"You've never heard from her since she passed?"

"Not even a peep."

"Sometimes intense emotions make it more difficult to get through," Estelle observed. Kat had felt her enter the room a split second before she spoke and was already turning to confirm the suspicion that Estelle knew more than she was saying.

"You've been in contact with her all along," Kat accused. "That's how you found me in the first place."

"Let's just say we found a mutually beneficial way to help our granddaughters." Judging by the self-satisfied look on her face, Estelle was not interested in forgiveness for her meddling ways. "She's quite a force, your grandmother. The name Zephyr suited her well."

"She could have just contacted me herself." Anger and resentment swirled like poison seeping into Kat's bones.

"There are a few things I'd like to say to her."

"Have a care before you start slinging blame around like knives, young Kat." Estelle shook a finger of warning, and when she spoke, there was steel in her voice. "You can't fault someone for a genetic predisposition. She had no more choice than you did in receiving sensitivity as her birthright. Now that you can see, it is time for you to begin looking.

"Riddles, Estelle?"

"There's a locked box in the second bedroom closet. The key is in the kitchen; she says you'll know where. Open the box and learn about the woman you thought you knew." With a last wagging of her finger, Estelle was gone.

"Guess I'm not the only one who got on Estelle's bad side," Amethyst commented, hoping to lighten the mood.

Inevitably, the topic of dating came up, and considering everyone else was matched up, Kat's first date became the centerpiece of the conversation.

"Disaster—of King Kong-like proportions. I thought you were exaggerating about how bad it could be, but I was wrong—so wrong." Kat shook her head. "How am I supposed to take a guy seriously when his dead aunt tells me all his childhood secrets? He's probably a really nice guy, but between his family butting in and him freaking out over what I do, it was an epic fail."

"Wait here." Gustavia's long legs flashed under a slim confection of a skirt that just skimmed her ankles. Sewn out of cloth from her own design, she'd found a website offering printed fabric using any image of her choice. Today it was a water scene complete with pink flamingos.

Moments later, she returned with a gaudy plastic tiara, popped it on Kat's head, and announced, "Welcome to the club. Here's your tiara. Wear it with pride."

"There's more, though." They were going to tease her, Kat knew, but in the end, they would also help. Still, she was embarrassed to admit, "I figured out that I don't know how to flirt." When her statement was met with neither laughter nor sympathy, she shrugged off the feelings of uneasiness, "I mean, I knew how when I was fourteen, but it can't be the same, right?"

Whatever she had expected, it had not been the glint of an accepted challenge mirrored across three faces. Why did she feel like she had just started a game of Whack the Hornet's Nest?

"Show us," Julie commanded.

Face flaming red, Kat wished she had just Googled it instead. "It was nothing," she muttered, "just a smile and a hair twirl."

"Show us," Gustavia, a huge grin on her face, waved a hand to indicate that Kat should get on with it. Friends like these were a blessing—mostly.

"I'll be the guy." Amethyst volunteered. She lowered her already deep voice another octave or two, effected what she considered a manly swagger, strolled across the room, leaned over, and gave Kat an obvious up and down look, "Hey, baby. How's it going?"

It was too much for Kat, who burst into peals of laughter.

Amethyst couldn't have looked less like a man. She was wearing a simple sheath dress in a color that nearly perfectly matched the new shade of her hair, topped with a garment loosely crocheted from some fuzzy type of yarn that was not quite a sweater but not quite a cape in a deeper purple tone.

Expressive eyes under a sweep of long, thick lashes—several blended tones of brown shading their lids—framed by a swing of blunt-cut hair were utterly feminine. When Amethyst chose a signature color, she gave herself to it with abandon. The tiny woman almost always reminded Kat of a woodland fairy.

"No, let me." Gustavia was even less masculine in pink and bottle-green, with no fewer than eight beaded necklaces draped around her neck. When she waggled her eyebrows and gave an exaggerated head toss, Kat shook her head. "No, please. Just don't. There's no way I can do this. Absolutely. No. Way."

"Want me to get Tyler? He'd make a better guy than the two of you." Julie frowned, "Wait, that didn't come out right." Her words cracked them all up again.

Finally, Amethyst sobered up. She didn't need to see the muddied colors of Kat's aura to know there was more going on here than just a bit of insecurity. Kat had chosen to cut herself off from certain rites of passage—Prom, that fumbling first kiss, stepping on his toes during an awkward slow dance. Ahead of her still lay so many firsts that most women remembered for the rest of their lives and that most men of a certain age never expected to be part of again. No wonder she was nervous.

What Kat needed was for them to pass on their collective wisdom and help smooth the path for her. It was a sacred duty, and once Amethyst understood that the last lingering vestige of laughter fell away.

This was no laughing matter; this was more like a sacred charge.

Amethyst sat on the table in front of Kat, ignored Julie's pointed look about sitting on furniture not made for the purpose, and took hold of Kat's hand. Then, she did her best Yoda imitation. "Hmmm. Dating wisdom, so you want to know."

Okay, fine. It was a serious situation, but there was no reason not to have a little fun with it. Kat would probably feel more at ease if things stayed on the lighter side. She ignored Kat's rolling eyeballs and Julie's snort behind her and jumped in.

"Did your mother ever tell you boys only want one thing?"

"No."

"Well, good. Because it's not true. Men want lots of things, mostly the same things you want. Love, companionship, someone to grow old with, someone who understands them. The whole package." Behind her, Julie and Gustavia nodded in agreement. "Just as long as the whole package includes plenty of that one thing."

"Flirting hasn't changed that much from when you were fourteen..." Gustavia broke in, "...because half the men you meet will still have—on a hormonal level anyway—a teenager in their pants," her interruption garnering her a quick grin from Amethyst.

Julie had also picked up on what was at the heart of Kat's problem. She was having a *13 Going on 30* moment, which had less to do with flirting than knowing what to expect. "Just be yourself. Flirting is mostly a nonverbal way of letting a man know your level of interest. Making eye contact and smiling lets him know he has a shot at not being turned down whether he is asking for a first date or a third or to take things to the next level."

"How will I know if I'm going too far? You know, what's the difference between *I like your smile* and *take me here on the table?*"

"Sadly, the only way to learn is by experience."

"It's true," Gustavia agreed, "trial by fire and speaking of, I gave your number to a guy I met at my dentist's office. Just my way of adding a little kindling."

CHAPTER NINE

Dufus. Do people still say dufus? Doesn't matter. It's the best word to describe Kevin. Only a dufus would take a woman to dinner and bring his parents on a first date. Kat's mind had been running on this track all during appetizers.

Then, when she learned his mother was a psychologist who was inordinately interested in everything to do with how Kat had come to be blind and how she had restored her vision, she decided Gustavia's matchmaking days were over.

"And your parents? How do they feel about what has happened to you?" Kevin's father had not said a word yet, but his mother would not stop asking personal questions.

"They're thrilled. If you don't mind, I need a moment."

Excusing herself, Kat grabbed her purse and hurried toward the restroom. After pulling out her phone, she was walking and typing a 911 text to order Gustavia to ride to the rescue when she rounded the corner toward the restroom and rammed full force into someone coming the other way. Inattentive woman meets immovable object. Kat bounced back a step from the impact.

Trying to get her breath back, she opened her mouth to apologize, "I'm sorry, I wasn't watching where I was...." And looking up, found herself staring into a pair of familiar brown eyes.

"Zack. I didn't expect to run into you here—literally." Kat smiled, hoping he would be a gentleman and give her a ride home.

"Kevin Hale, huh? I wouldn't have pegged him for being your type." The chill in his voice surprised Kat; she frowned.

"I have a type?" Did two dates in a lifetime translate into someone having a type? She didn't think so. "What's wrong with Kevin?" And how did I end up in a position to defend the man when all I really wan to do is get away from him and his mother? That last, she refrained from saying out loud.

"He's an accountant, very down to earth."

"What's that supposed to mean?" Maybe she wouldn't ask for that ride home after all. What had gotten into him? He was not acting like himself.

He ignored the question. "His father has the personality of a wet dishrag, and his mother is a psychologist who volunteers with a troubled youth program in the city."

"I'm aware of that since he brought them both on our date, and she's spent twenty minutes grilling me about how I feel now that I can see again." She couldn't keep the exasperation from slipping into her voice. "I had no idea I'd been the topic of so much gossip."

"Wow, how long have you been seeing him?" Why hadn't he heard about this? Meeting the parents? That's a big step.

"It's our first date." The flood of irrational annoyance drained out of him, leaving amusement in its place.

"Who brings their parents on a first date?"

"I've been asking myself that very same question. I was just texting your sister to see if she could help me pull a Houdini. I don't think I can face going back to that table, but I don't want to be rude."

He took pity on her. "Go back, give me two minutes, and I'll rescue you. Whatever I say, just go with it." He'd have to miss dinner with his own parents, but that was a common enough occurrence given the unpredictability of his line of work. A quick stop at their table to say hello, and then he could save Kat from her woeful dilemma.

As Zack approached her table, he knew the moment she sensed his approach. Trained to observe, he noted the subtle change in her posture, the slight turn of her head that let her eyes slide toward him, then the way she relaxed in relief.

With a wicked glint in his eye, he decided to make a show of it. No way would Kevin be getting a second date. Zack cast a fulminating look at the man, ignoring how justified it felt, and stepped up beside Kat, who looked up at him in feigned surprise.

"What are you doing here with him?" Zack all but growled the words, then turned his head to slip Kat a wink on the sly.

"What do you care? You didn't call me for a week, so I thought it was over." She shrugged and struggled to keep from smiling.

"If I decide it's over, believe me, you'll know."

Kat pasted a disgusted look on her face, "Welcome to the new millennium, where women are allowed to have opinions." She stood up and faced him, toe-to-toe. "What? You thought I would sit at home and wait for you to swoop in whenever you felt like it? Sorry, not happening. Now if you don't mind..." Kat tossed her head to indicate he should leave. Out of the corner of her eye, she could see Kevin and his parents squirming in their seats.

"Oh baby, you know it wasn't like that. I got busy at work,

and time just slipped away. You know you're my pookie-bear. Come on. Come with me now. Please?"

There would be sore places tomorrow where she had to bite her cheek to keep from giggling.

"Ok, snuggly-ugums." She turned to Kevin, "I'm sorry. You don't mind, do you?" Before he even had time to answer, Kat grabbed her purse and linking her arm with Zack's, the two of them turned and made it all the way out the door before the first burst of laughter escaped.

"Pookie-bear?" Kat wheezed and doubled over.

"Snuggly-ugams? Did you see the look on his face?"

"No, I didn't dare to look."

"I don't think we fooled his mother, though."

"I don't care; it was her underhanded way of doing research for a book she's writing about how people cope with tragedy." Suddenly, Kat didn't find the experience quite as amusing. "She could have just asked, I would have talked to her about it, but this was beyond the pale."

Grasping her arm companionably, Zack led her toward the parking lot and his car. No police cruiser tonight; he was driving one of those compact hybrids that ran on gas or electricity. Gustavia wasn't the only one in the family concerned with the environment.

Without thinking much about it, Kat rested her hand on Zack's, where it curved against her arm. His guard was down, and without that prickly exterior, she felt very safe around him. Protected.

Being a gentleman, he opened the door and waited to close it behind her. She glanced around the car's interior, expecting it to be utilitarian but was surprised to find it comfortable though not overly luxurious. She detected a hint of new car smell.

It wasn't until Zack had circled back to the driver's side and slid into his seat that she realized he had just put aside whatever plans he'd had to take care of her.

"Oh, I'm sorry. Did I just ruin a date? I'll call Julie or Gustavia and wait here. Go back inside and have your dinner." Kat laid a hand on his arm and gave a little push to add emphasis. "I didn't mean to derail your plans." A tiny wisp of envy rose inside her at the thought of him on a date.

"No, it's fine. My parents have a standing dinner date here every other week, and I join them whenever I can. It's no big deal."

It would have been a big deal to his sister, who had been, until recently, on the fringe of her own family dynamic—partly by choice and partly based on a series of secrets and misunderstandings. All of that had been cleared up, but Kat felt surprisingly defensive on the part of her friend.

"What about Gustavia? Is she invited to these dinners, or will she be left out again?"

"Sheath the claws, Kitty Kat. It's a family thing; she's obviously family, so she shows up when she can."

Calling her Kitty Kat garnered him a raised eyebrow, but she let it go and settled back in her seat.

"Speaking of dinner, we've missed ours. I could go for a slice of meatloaf." He glanced over at her, "You up for it? I know a little pub that does this killer gourmet version. But I warn you. It's addictive."

"I've already ruined your rep in front of Kevin. Are you sure you want to be seen with me in another public venue?"

"Have a heart. I'm half-starved. Wasting away to nothing." His stomach gave a loud grumbling noise to prove the point.

Casting an eye over his muscular form, she doubted he was in any immediate danger but decided to take pity on him anyway. "Take me to the meatloaf, but if you call me Pookie Bear again, retaliation will be swift and painful.

One hand companionably grasping hers, Zack led Kat into Hang. Housed between a barbershop and an auto parts store, the pub seemed out of place in the short, brick-fronted row of connected businesses.

If the smell was anything to go by, the food would be as good as promised, probably explaining why Zack was a regular visitor. That much was obvious the minute they walked through the door.

A man about the size of a small bear, nearly as hairy and probably just as strong, barked out, "Hey Roman," and stepped around the bar to greet Zack with a brutal-looking handshake and a clap on the back that might have knocked a smaller man to his knees before turning his attention on Kat.

Feeling slightly overwhelmed when the big man turned toward her, a welcoming grin on his face, Kat could see that the smile lines around his eyes were deeply etched. He held out a hand the size of a baseball mitt and introduced himself, "Name's Kane, and you are?" He eyed her speculatively, then glanced over at Zack.

"I'm Kat." Was all she had time for before he yanked her into a hug, lifting her nearly off her feet, and planted a great smacking kiss on her cheek.

Zack grinned and watched Kane urge Kat onto a stool at the bar before bellowing toward the kitchen area at the rear of the small pub. "Molly, get out here and see what Zack's brought with him."

"Be out in a minute," yelled a feminine voice, her words punctuated by the rattling of some pans.

"Hey, Moll, got any meatloaf back there?" Zack called back to her.

"Course I do. I'll bring you a plate."

"Bring two."

"Two?" Judging from the surprised inflection, Kat felt she

was about to fall under intense scrutiny.

"You'll sit here and keep me company," Kane pronounced before stepping back to draw a foaming pitcher of beer and deposit it on the nearest table. "Unless you want a table, something cozy in the back?" The big man put a lot of innuendo into the question.

"Right here will be just fine," Kat spoke from her bar stool before Zack could answer. Tonight he had given her a glimpse of the playful man under the mask of responsible authority he normally wore. Curious to learn more about both, she thought Kane might be an excellent source of information. It was obvious there was more than good customer relations between them.

"How do you know Zack? Did you grow up together?"

Kane's belly laugh startled Kat with its sudden noise.

"Not exactly," and then the burly man went on to explain how a misspent youth had ended when Zack arrested him and then, seeing something in the younger man, helped him get into a program that included a course in culinary arts. He'd met the irrepressible Molly, and the rest was history.

Kat swiveled on her stool to get a better look at the place. Small but with plenty of atmosphere. Gleaming wood trim scaled slightly large for the size of the room, cleverly framed sections of wall painted in a rich red color. Within the framed areas hung musical instruments and lush, green landscapes.

The bar was situated in the long part of the L-shaped room just far enough away from the small, cleared area around the corner where a young man played his guitar and sang earnestly that the music made a pleasant backdrop but did not overpower conversation.

Kat's belly wrenched and complained at its emptiness as mouth-watering odors continued to waft from the kitchen.

She didn't have long to wait before Molly swung out of the

back carrying a huge tray with several plates on it. Stashing it on the end of the bar, the tiny woman made short work of serving fragrant meals to a couple seated at the closest table while Kane passed Zack and Kat a little bit of heaven.

A huge slab of meatloaf studded with bits of bell pepper, onion, and mushroom, then drenched in tangy homemade ketchup and topped with two crunchy, hand-dipped onion rings shared the plate with a mound of creamy, chive-infused mashed potatoes and carrots glistening in an orange, maple, and ginger glaze.

No wonder Zack was addicted to this place.

Out of the corner of his eye, Zack watched with interest as Kat ate slowly but with great relish. Granted, his experience had been somewhat limited—surprising how many women thought cops made bad dating prospects—but he had never seen a woman on a date eat with such enjoyment. After the first bite, she closed her eyes and nearly hummed with pleasure.

Kane introduced Molly, who eyed Kat with friendly speculation. Refusing to be intimidated, Kat returned her assessing gaze. By any standards, Molly would be considered petite, but standing next to Kane, she appeared positively elfin. Her nearly-white pixie-cut hair over emerald green eyes in a face liberally dusted in freckles only drew more attention to her small stature. Put her in a pinafore and curls, and she would have made the perfect Goldilocks next to Kane's bearlike size.

Amethyst might actually feel tall standing next to her.

Before she could help herself, Kat pointed her fork toward Molly, "So, did you two meet over a bowl of porridge?" popped out of her mouth, and Zack barked out a laugh.

Embarrassed color washed over Kat's face, but before she could apologize, both Kane and Molly started to laugh as well.

"Good one. Where'd you find her?" Molly directed the question at Zack, putting him on the spot with a wickedly raised eyebrow and revealing her roots as there was more than a touch of Ireland in her voice.

"Friend of my sister's," he mumbled.

"Interesting. What's she like?" Kane demanded of Kat, "Gustavia, I mean. Zack refuses to bring her by."

That earned the man a punch in the shoulder. "Are you ashamed of her? Still? That's disappointing."

"Ow, give me some credit." Zack rubbed the sore spot where she had smacked him and thought she had packed a decent punch. "I was afraid these two would embarrass me by asking for her autograph or something. They're star-struck."

"It's us he's ashamed of, then," Molly observed, then turned back to Kat. "Tell me about her. Does she really dress like she does in the photos on her book jackets?"

"Yes, she really does. You're familiar with her work, then?"

"I've a niece who is positively obsessed with the woman. Offered Zack six months' worth of free food to bring her around, but he thinks he's playing the protective brother."

Now it was Zack's face that turned a dull red. "I didn't want her to think I was using her for free food." Then Kat knew it went deeper. He was still unsure how Gustavia would react if he asked for a favor. The years of separation between the siblings had taken its toll on him, too.

Laying a sympathetic hand on his arm where it still smarted from her blow, she ignored the shot of molten heat that seared at the brief contact and affirmed, "Gustavia would be thrilled if you asked her. She loves to meet her readers, but more than that, she would be touched that you included her in your life."

Kat asked Molly, "Do I get free meatloaf if I bring her in?"

Zack chuckled, "You'll have to beat me to it. Why don't you tell Molly what you do for a living?" If she could poke into his personal life, he could poke into hers.

If he thought she would be embarrassed, he was way off the

73

mark. "I read Tarot cards and sometimes connect the living with those who have passed on."

Molly breathed. "Ahh, you've the sight, then. Just like my Mam. She had a canny way with her."

"It was my grandmother who passed it on to me."

"Skipped over your mum, then?"

Unsettled, Kat realized she had never asked but had always assumed that if her mother had had personal experience, she would have offered more or better advice.

To keep from dwelling on the subject, Kat added, "I'm thinking of taking some classes in the fall, though. Up until..." she paused to decide how much she wanted to reveal, "I was a teenager when I started seeing spirits, and until then, I planned to become a librarian."

Zack snorted and then choked, trying not to spray beer all over his food. Kat had to whack him on the back until he regained the ability to speak. "A librarian?"

"Why? What's wrong with that?"

"Nothing. Just unexpected, is all." Great, now he saw sexy librarian images featuring Kat in the role floating around in his head.

Molly watched the exchange with pleasure while Kane moved around the small area behind the bar to draw more drinks. Her kitchen staff could handle that end of things without her for the next little while; this was too interesting to pass up.

"And just what were you expecting?"

"You don't want to keep giving readings?" He countered.

"I can do both. Don't get me wrong, giving readings allowed me a lot more independence than I ever thought possible, but having this ability was a choice made for me. I'd like the chance to try something else that interests me. Pigeonholes are for pigeons."

Now she turned the conversation back on him, "What about you? Did you always want to be a cop?"

By his hesitation, she could tell the question touched a nerve.

"I was supposed to follow in my father's footsteps and, failing that, in my mother's. They found it disappointing that I had no interest in politics and even less in the medical profession."

When the conversation turned personal, Molly decided to give Zack some privacy, so she fetched a damp rag and some cleanser to begin wiping down nearby tables. All the while keeping her ears sharp for any good gossip.

"They must be proud of you, though."

"They've come to terms with it since it was the lesser of two evils to them. Dad considers it a stepping stone to greater things, and Mom has been happier since I chose to take the position here in Oakville. Safer than being a cop in the city."

"Lesser of two evils—what was the other choice?"

"A topic for another day. Can't reveal all my secrets on the first date."

Date? He thought this was a date? Butterflies took flight in her stomach, and her mouth went dry. Objectively, this was the best first date she had been on so far. Good food, decent conversation, and that delicious tingle every time his arm brushed against hers.

"...get to know my sister better."

Uh oh, he'd been talking while she was off in her own little space reacting to his date comment.

"Gustavia is one of the best people I know. She didn't deserve all that family drama." He sensed her disapproval and knew he had earned it for his part in things. "Without her help, I don't think I would have been able to live by myself. My folks have been super supportive and pushed me to be as independent as possible with everyday tasks." Throwing her normal desire for privacy out the window, Kat continued to explain.

"Gustavia helped me refine some of the systems I relied on, but mostly she dragged me out of my shell at every possible opportunity. It's hard to explain, but she found that balance between being helpful and forcing me to do more than I thought possible." Kat blinked at the sting of tears. "And all without making me feel like a burden."

He let her talk it out.

"Like my clothes..." she lifted the hem on her sweater to show him a small, round button sewn on the inside, "...round buttons for blue, square for red, and oblong for yellow. Add a second button for secondary colors, so it would be a round and a square button for purple. Gustavia took the idea and refined it even more. She added a third button to let me know that a shade of green might have more blue than yellow in it and then instituted the bead system."

"Glass beads for items that needed to be dry cleaned, plastic for wash and wear. And being Gustavia, she took it another step. She sorted everything by what could go together and for what purpose and used various shapes so I knew I could put on any two items with faceted beads and look fine for a dressed up occasion, round beads for white, square beads for black."

"I missed out on a lot of years with her." Zack spoke quietly, "every time I hear a story like this, I feel that cost even deeper. At least she had friends like you." The hand he laid over hers for a quick squeeze might have been made from lightning for the jolt it gave her.

Best first date so far.

CHAPTER TEN

The second bedroom nestled into the eaves of Kat's house was full of memories. How many nights had she cuddled under the covers listening to her grandmother talk to friends around the dining room table? It only occurred to her now that those friends might not all have been among the living.

With only a single morning appointment and the afternoon free, today was as good a time as any to look for the box Estelle had told her to find.

How much smaller the room looked since the last time she had sat on the floor to sort through old photographs stored in the bottom dresser drawer. Her favorites were the ones from the seventies when the men wore colorful polyester suits and long sideburns. There was one of her dad wearing a powder blue leisure suit with brown stitching that always brought a smile.

Stalling, she pulled open the drawer to leaf through the stack for it. She would carry it like a talisman when she went into the closet to find whatever was hidden there amid the old rolls of wallpaper, spare blankets, and boxes of things still unsorted after all the years since her grandmother had passed.

Maybe her mother had been unable to face the job, or maybe she had been waiting for Kat to help her. After all, she had been the only one still convinced, even after the years continued to pass, that her daughter would one day regain what had been lost.

Whatever the reason, the closet remained as it had always been. Kat felt a sense of nostalgia as she pulled the string to switch on the overhead light and looked into the darkest corner where the ceiling slanted down low. She would have to duck or crawl to get back into the shadowed depths where she knew the box was hiding.

No time like the present. Whatever the big secret, Kat needed to know. She had just flicked on the flashlight when she heard the door close downstairs and her mother's voice. "Kathleen, are you here?"

"Upstairs, Mom. I'm in the little bedroom closet."

Perfect timing. Suspiciously perfect, actually.

"I was just about to start sorting through some things in here." She announced as her mother entered the room. "Want to help?"

If there was anything to hide, Anne Canton managed it masterfully. Her face remained open and cheerful as she offered her daughter a hug. "I'd forgotten there were still things stored up here. Your grandmother was a bit of a pack rat."

Kat had not intended to empty the closet but could not pass up the opportunity to spend time with her mother. Sharing this task gave her a deep sense of connectedness that had been lacking for a long time.

By the time Anne happened upon the box, Kat had forgotten it was the reason they were digging around in the past, to begin with. "Look at this," Anne carried the box into the bedroom,

"It's locked. I wonder if there's a key somewhere." She angled the box to look at it curiously, then passed it to Kat, who reached for it.

"There is. Follow me." Kat carried the box down to the kitchen, where she set it gently on the table before stretching to take down the teapot with the sugar and creamer attached. "I'm pretty sure this will fit." Her quick fingers retrieved the little key from among the rubber bands and twist ties. She passed it over to let her mother test it in the lock.

Whatever she had been expecting to find, handbills with photos of a beautiful young woman wearing period ballet dancer garb had not been on the list. "Is that grandmother?"

Anne took a closer look. "It is." A quick intake of breath. "She looks so young, so happy."

"Did you know she'd been a dancer?" Kat continued to leaf through the box. There was a newspaper article about a girl named Nora, a local ballerina, being accepted into one of the most prestigious corps in the country. There were cards and letters of congratulation, dried rose petals presumably from an opening night bouquet. Then a second article with the story detailing how a promising young dancer, predicted to become prima, had walked away from the stage to disappear into obscurity.

Kat felt a chill right before hearing her mother say, "You could have told me, you know." She whirled to see Anne wagging a finger at the spirit of her grandmother. "You," Kat pointed her own, "You can see spirit, and you never said a word."

"I'm afraid it's my fault. I knew I'd passed my gift on to your mother when she started talking to her Uncle John almost as soon as she learned to speak, but as she grew older, the ability seemed to have faded away."

"It didn't fade. Not exactly." Anne confessed something she

had never told anyone. Not even her own mother. "A spirit or an angel came to me and said I could choose to see or not, and I chose not." She turned to her mother, "I'd forgotten it ever happened until you decided to become Madame Zephyr."

"When your father passed, I needed to make a living, and since it was my only marketable skill…"

Anne turned to Kat, "There was no sign that you had the sight, so we assumed it had skipped a generation until it hit you all at once. Then, we lost your grandmother before she could help you learn to control it."

"You still could have told me, and how is it you're seeing her now?"

Her grandmother answered, "Special dispensation from an angel named…"

"Galmadriel," Kat finished for her. "Is she around? I'd like to know why no one ever offered me that choice." Bitterness twisted her emotions into a greasy knot of anger.

"Nor was I," Nora offered in a mild rebuke. "Though I believe Anne paid the price for her decision, did you not?" She turned to her daughter.

"Do you think it was easy to watch you trying to deal with what happened after knowing I had turned my back on the one thing that would have helped you the most? If I had retained my gift, I could have helped you understand yours." Tears filled Anne's eyes. "Can you ever forgive me?"

Kat couldn't stand to see her mother cry. "Of course. Don't cry, mommy, please." She hugged Anne tightly while Nora watched.

"Grandmother, why did you walk away from dancing? Did your gift develop late in life as well?"

"No, but something else was developing. You see, I'd met this handsome young man who called me his Zephyr because he thought I floated across the stage on the back of a western wind. He was quite a poet, your grandfather. Keep digging in that box, and you'll find out for yourself."

"He followed me across the country from performance to performance. When the company was slated to go to Europe, he swore he would follow me there, but by then, Anne was more than just a twinkle in his eye, so we settled down here in Oakville and started a life together."

"I've never heard that story before. Didn't you miss the ballet?"

"Annie, it has always been your nature to take on the world's pain. I was afraid you might feel responsible for my choices. I loved to dance, but I loved your father and the family he gave me so much more."

"Now, back to the business at hand. My time runs short. Kathleen, you perceive your time of darkness as a sign of weakness because some twit of a doctor with no experience in the matter called it so. This is an untruth and an unkind one at that."

Kat raised both eyebrows in surprise.

"Tell me this, how clearly do you see and hear me right now?"

"As clearly as I see and hear any living person. Why? Is that not normal?"

Nora smiled, "All I ever saw were misty, indistinct flashes of figures. But then I was mostly only clairsentient. I received signs, symbols, and feelings. Don't get me wrong, I was very good at interpreting those messages, but I never heard spirit speak directly to me. Your blindness forced you to develop clairaudience as a second ability, so you went from seeing distinct presences to hearing them clearly as well. It's quite remarkable."

"You're telling me my blindness was not a form of psychosis? A subconscious response to fear?" An unbelievable weight lifted from Kat. It had been a constant worry to her that any fright might cause a relapse or that she might pass some type of genetic response to fear along to her own children should she choose to have any.

"Absolutely not. Fear may have played a part in lengthening the experience, but not in causing it."

Kat felt anger creeping back, "And you couldn't have shown up here before now to let me know? Maybe speed up the process, make it a little easier on me?"

"Yes, mother, why now?" Anne demanded.

"Special dispensation. Galmadriel is busy elsewhere and asked Estelle to handle this, but I begged to be the one to come and explain, to have the chance to spend just a little more time with my girls. Oh, Annie, I'm so proud of you. Of both of you. It takes a strong woman to go against every instinct and force your child to stand on her own when all you want to do is protect. Look what you did for Kat; I know exactly what it cost you. The tears you've cried in private were never tears cried alone. I was always beside you."

"Thank you," Annie whispered, her voice rough with emotion.

"And Kathleen, trees grow the strongest roots when they are clinging to rocky soil. I hope you won't allow bitterness to taint your experience because then it will have all been for nothing. There are many paths open to you; don't let anger blind you from seeing them."

With a final smile and a longing look, Nora laid one hand on her heart, reached the other toward the two women standing before her, and faded away.

A heavy silence filled the room for a long time after Nora was gone. Kat opened her mouth several times to speak, but words wouldn't come. Still staring at the point where her mother had been standing, Anne finally mustered up the courage to ask, "Do you hate me?"

"Oh, Mom, no. How could I?"

"I should have told you."

"What difference would it have made? It changed nothing probably would have resented you for making the choice I would have made given the chance. At the time." When she made the qualification, Kat knew it was the truth.

"And now?"

"It wasn't "hysterical blindness," she spat the words as though bitter in her mouth, "that term has been hanging over my head like a wrecking ball because it made me feel like a victim who was too fragile to handle life. Yet, look around. I've done all right for myself, and I've helped a lot of people in the process."

Kat stood taller, "I think I'm okay with that.

CHAPTER ELEVEN

Only two blocks from the waterfront, Kat's street was one of the shortest in Oakville. It was also one of the most crowded. None of the properties qualified as historical, but as neighborhoods went, it was the oldest in the town's centralized area. A row of narrow houses painted in Easter egg colors with gingerbread trim lined both sides of a relatively short street.

The third house on the left painted a cheerful yellow with its bright blue door, white trim, and tiny picket fence, fit right in with the rest. Except for the words Madame Zephyr painted on a small sign, there was nothing about the house that screamed *a psychic lives here*, and even then, the sign barely whispered.

Most of Kat's business came from word-of-mouth advertising, and the rest she inherited from her grandmother, along with the house.

As he steered the little hybrid into her short drive, Zack thought he saw movement through the curtains. In a low voice, he said, "I thought you lived here alone."

"I do. Why?" Kat frowned.

"Then you have an unexpected guest. Wait here. I'll go

check it out."

But Kat had already recognized the figure inside from the shadow it cast behind the white eyelet window covering. Before she could catch up to him, he was already halfway to the door, and there was no way to warn her uninvited guests.

On a half run, she caught up and grabbed his arm. "No, it's finc. I know who it is. Nothing to worry about." But he'd seen the surprise in her eyes and was not fooled.

"Then you can introduce me because I'm not letting you go in alone."

No amount of argument changed his mind, so she unlocked the door with a sigh of resignation and stepped inside to key in the alarm code.

Zack could already hear voices, and one of them was male. Jealousy, like a bolt of lightning, slammed into his gut.

He should have been surprised by the feeling, but he wasn't.

Julie, forgive me, Kat thought to herself as she followed Zack into the dining room. Too close, she almost slammed into his back when he stopped short. In an instant, Zack felt jealousy die within him. Judging from the surprised looks mirrored on both faces, neither Estelle nor Julius had been expecting Zack to walk through the door. Estelle looked past him to Kat, who shrugged fatalistically. It was already too late to change the situation. Zack was about to meet a pair of nosy ghosts.

"Sorry to barge in like this..." he began, then his eyes widened as he recognized the woman sitting at the dining room table, "wait a minute. I saw you the night Gustavia was taken. You showed up at the bar to warn us. I wanted to thank you, but when I turned around, you were gone." The whole time he was speaking to Estelle, Zack's eyes kept darting past her to Julius. The man looked familiar, but his trained memory failed him for once, and he could not remember where he had seen that face before.

"Maybe you'd better sit down, Zack, and I'll introduce you."

Since the floorboards probably would not open up and swallow her whole, Kat decided the just-rip-off-the-Band-Aid approach was probably best. "I'd like you to meet Julie's grandmother Estelle, and this is her great-grandfather, Julius."

A dull silence fell over the room as Zack assessed the two entities seated at the table; Kat could see the wheels turning as his agile brain made connections and conclusions. When it fell into place for him, he pushed away from the table to stalk across the room, where he stared at a shelf lined with vintage teapots without seeing any of them. He ran a hand through his hair, making Kat wonder if it would feel as silky as it looked.

The tension coming off of Zack was palpable, his posture still and unyielding. Meanwhile, the two ghosts continued to sit calmly.

Suddenly he turned, "But you're…"

"Departed? Dead, deceased, mortally challenged, ti…toes up," Julius changed gears when Estelle's elbow jammed into his ribs, "yes, we are."

Twinkling eyes accompanied a slightly smug smile from Estelle when Zack said, "But I can see you."

Julius burst out, "About time, too." His voice seemed loud in the room. "Your young man, here, is the last part of the circle. I don't know how you expected to go on keeping him in the dark."

Kat took umbrage at the censure she detected behind his words and the insinuation that Zack belonged to her.

"We didn't think he could see you, so what would be the point in telling him we've been in contact with the pair of you all this time? He's nothing like Gustavia. His mind is closed."

That got his attention.

Zack turned to defend the part of his mind that was insisting

86

this could not be happening but found he had nothing to say. He remembered where he had seen this man before: immortalized in oil in that painting on Julie's mantel. In rapid fire, his mind produced several scenarios, each more implausible than the one before, for how or why anyone would go to these lengths to play out a hoax. Every option that came to mind was nothing more than a smokescreen to protect a willing suspension of disbelief. This was happening. It was real.

"Lay it out for me. The whole story," he commanded, the order proving his mind was not entirely closed. Kat had to give him credit for that much, anyway. The harp-backed wooden dining room chair thumped against the floor when Zack pulled it out somewhat forcefully and dropped into it.

"It all started when I died." Julius began.

"Do we really need to go back that far?" Kat thought the full narrative might be too much for Zack.

"It's important," Estelle assured her. To Julius, she said, "Try to keep it short, though."

As concisely as possible, Julius recounted the story of his spoiled son, Estelle's first husband Edward, and how he had felt it prudent to hide the majority of his valuables to keep them being squandered before they could be passed down to future generations. When he got to the part about how he had devised a treasure hunt of sorts to ensure that only an heir of sufficient intelligence would find the heirlooms, Kat hoped he would elaborate. There was still one cache left to find, and so far, Julius had provided no clues for Julie and her friends to follow.

She was doomed to disappointment because Julius only explained how his plan to leave a set of written clues had been derailed by his untimely demise.

"My last thoughts were regrets that I had not left Estelle enough information to follow through with, and then I was dead. But, when I tried to go into the light, something held me back, and I was stuck where I am now, halfway between the living world and the afterlife with that harpy of an angel shouting at me for being an idiot."

"Galmadriel?" Kat wondered.

"You talk to angels, too?" Zack wished he had a pin to poke himself with because he was sure pinching would not be enough to prove whether he was awake or dreaming.

"Not me, Amethyst." Kat gestured for Julius to continue despite Zack's incredulity.

"Is every spirit that visits me an earthwalker?"

"No," Julius looked away as he told an uncomfortable truth, "we could have contacted you just as easily from inside the light, but by the time I figured that out, the damage was already done."

Estelle took up the story. "Julius tried to contact me for years, but I was not sensitive enough to hear or see him. When I died and started to go into the light, he was there to explain things, but it took too long, and I missed my window, so I chose to stay and help."

"Thought the angel was going to explode. Seems that kind of thing just isn't done on the other side. I'm in a fair amount of trouble over it."

"We're both in trouble now, thanks to him, and as punishment, we're slated to become guardian angels."

Kat raised an eyebrow, "Punishment? Sounds more like a reward to me."

"Not according to Galmadriel. She says they plan to assign us to the most hapless humans they can find for the first five centuries or so."

"Fair enough, sounds like a perfect fit to me." Kat wondered, "Does that mean Galmadriel is Amethyst's guardian angel?"

Estelle and Julius exchanged an uncomfortable look.

"Not exactly. Galmadriel has other duties, but she got dragged into our drama because she happened to be around at the time. None of us counted on Logan or the earthwalker getting involved."

There was more, Kat sensed.

Throughout Estelle's telling of the story, Julius grew paler and quieter until he burst out, "It was all my fault. I should have gone into the light, and when I didn't, the doorway held open longer than it should have. Billy must have been hovering around, hoping for just such an occurrence because that's how he managed to navigate his way to the living world by pulling extra strength from the light. With his grudge against my family and his blood connection to Logan, he picked exactly the right time and place."

Kat was confused. "Pulling strength from the light?"

"Earthwalkers are spirits who deliberately turn from the light. Technically, I am one, as is Estelle."

His words shocked Kat.

"But you two are not evil." This much she knew without question.

"Only because our intentions were good, and as long as we stick to those intentions, we'll be fine. Over time, the temptation to meddle enough to alter someone's free will gets stronger, and even our intentions might not be protection enough. Most spirits never make it that long. They see reason after a generation or two and find their way back to the light. Others never wanted the light to begin with, and few, like Billy, find a human host, and at that point, they are beyond redemption."

The concept was a lot to digest. Kat needed time to ponder the implications, but Julius had another bombshell to drop.

"Billy is intentionally killing Logan from the inside, and unless the earthwalker leaves willingly or is forced into the void before it is too late, Logan's soul will be ripped away."

How could Julius be telling her these things? Until now, he had been prevented by what he called "the powers that be" from giving out any of this kind of information. Something had obviously changed. There was more to the story. She was sure of it.

"Tell me the rest."

Estelle picked up where Julius left off, saying, "When Julie used the first key, she set in motion certain events. Whether or not she finds the final key, Julius and I can only stay until the equinox. At that point, if we have helped resolve the situation we caused, we will become guardian angels." Estelle closed her eyes and took the ghostly equivalent of a deep breath.

A chill settled over Kat, raising a few goosebumps on Zack's arms. "And if the situation has not been resolved? What happens then?"

"Our fate becomes bound to Billy's."

"What does that mean?"

"We will be tasked with carrying him forcefully into the void where our own souls will be lost forever."

For a moment, Kat could not speak; her brain was reluctant to process such dire information. Estelle's revelation was so shocking that no response seemed adequate.

She looked over at Zack, who sat back in his chair, arms crossed, face blank and unreadable. She would have attempted to soothe him at any other time, but not today. He was a big boy; he could take care of himself.

When he finally spoke, Kat got her second shock of the day.

"This Billy, the earthwalker, or whatever—" he shook his head, "what happens to Ellis if you take him to the void." He might as well have made air quotes considering the emphasis he gave the word.

It was Julius who spoke, his voice subdued, "If there is

anything of Ellis left by then, he will live. Otherwise…"

"Then we need a plan." Zack pulled out his phone, activated the note-taking app, and began to grill Julius for every bit of information the ghost could provide before Julius' energy level dropped too low for him to stay visible. There was no way he was letting Ellis slide off into some void without paying for his crimes.

Gesturing for Estelle to follow her, Kat went to the kitchen to make coffee. Perfectly dark roasted beans whirled in the grinder and perfumed the air with their earthy scent. Kat inhaled gratefully. The way this day was shaping up, she would need the caffeine boost. She may not have known Zack for years, but there was no mistaking his determination—before this night was over, he would have a plan. He'd probably have a few choice words for his sister, Kat, and the rest of the group for keeping so many secrets, too.

Easily the largest room in the house, the kitchen sprawled across the entire rear third of the first floor. Handcrafted cabinets coated with layer after layer of white paint stretched to the high ceiling; any little chip revealing age like the rings of a tree. Above the sink, a jalousie window faced the small backyard. Kat hadn't seen the area in so long that she had no idea whether any of the shrubs currently hibernating under a liberal coating of snow would flower in the spring.

Almost everything in the room belonged to another era. Kat's grandmother, the original Madame Zephyr, would have recognized everything in the room except for the gleaming, triple-priming, stainless steel espresso machine that looked like it would be more at home in the Jetson's kitchen.

Now that her sight had returned for good, Kat thought she might change the decor. Maybe add some items of her choosing to personalize the space more.

Once the hissing machine had dispensed its fragrant nectar,

Kat turned to Estelle, who had remained uncharacteristically quiet. "How is it that Julius is suddenly so free with the information?"

Estelle shrugged and tried to pull off a bit of nonchalance, but Kat wasn't having any of it.

"Time is running out, and with the circle complete..."

"You mean Zack?" Kat did not need to see Estelle's nod. She already knew he would be integral to their success. "How is it you've never mentioned this circle thing before? I mean, Julius had no way of knowing Julie would be the one to find his lost valuables when he created the hiding places and their keys."

"No, he didn't. Galmadriel set the parameters for the circle once Billy came into the picture. The way I understand it, she cannot influence Logan or any of the rest of you directly because that would interfere with your free will. But, she can work within an if-then scenario to enhance the chance for success."

Kat thought she caught a glimmer of Estelle's meaning, but the faint sense of understanding slid away before she could fully grasp it. She waited for the ghost to expand on the concept.

"In this case, the if-then was: If these eight people come together at this particular time and form a tight bond—then she could use the energy created by that bond to enhance their individual gifts."

"Thus increasing our chance for success." Brow furrowed, a thoughtful Kat mused, then looked more closely at the spirit. Everything about Estelle spoke of tension. From the strained lines across her forehead and around her eyes to the tightness of her jaw and gentle roundness of her shoulders told Kat there was still more to the story.

With no physical means of soothing the spirit, Kat's only

option was to get Estelle to open up and, by sharing her burden, ease some of the apprehension.

"Estelle, please…it's obvious something more is going on." She poured another cup of coffee, "The powers that be, as Julius calls them, have allowed you to speak with more detail than ever before—and about things you've been prevented from revealing in the past. Time is running out, and holding back won't make this any easier."

Kat wished she could do something, anything, to soothe away the misery that hung over Estelle like a lowering thundercloud.

"It's all our fault."

"What is?"

"All of it. Billy's connection to Julius led him to Logan, and his connection to Logan made it too easy for him to take over. He's hurt Gustavia, tried to hurt you. Amethyst has taken on a burden that she doesn't even understand yet, and all because of us. I let Julius talk me into staying to see Julie through, and look what happened."

"Yes," Kat agreed, "Look what happened. Julie is happily married to the man of her dreams and living in a house she can now afford to maintain. Gustavia is about to become engaged—that's a secret, by the way. Finn plans to ask her over Valentine's day. Amethyst has reunited with her husband, and I've regained my sight. You're horrible, meddlesome ghosts. I blame you for everything that's happened."

At her teasing tone, Estelle perked up a little. "I suppose there have been some benefits, and I trust you will all make the right choices when the time comes."

"All of our lives have changed for the better—well—except for Logan's, and we'll do what we can to fix that."

It was all she had to offer, all any of them had to offer. It would have to be enough. Estelle felt as though a weight had fallen from her. Turning twinkling eyes on Kat, "That man in the other room is very special—how are things going?"

Hot and red, Kat blushed, then cursed her fair skin. "It's not...I'm not...I don't know. My experience with men has been limited to teenage crushes, a couple of truly bad dates, and Zack."

"Just remember, my dear, he came in here to protect you, and then he stayed when meeting us went against everything he ever believed. His heart is as big as Gustavia's even if he hides it under bluster and a sense of duty."

"That's just his cop instincts. It wasn't personal."

Estelle rolled her eyes. Kat could feel her energy flagging and assumed Julius was also feeling the strain. Returning to the dining room, she found the pair of them finalizing some details on whatever plan they had cooked up. Julius was looking a bit transparent.

As he faded out completely, he instructed Kat to alert the others, and then it was just the two living persons left in the room.

"Coffee?" Kat offered as Zack continued typing into his phone. He looked up briefly and, to her amazement, smiled.

"Sure."

After Estelle's pep talk, Kat was even more unnerved by his larger-than-life presence and more so by his reaction to meeting her uninvited guests.

"You seem fairly calm, given what just happened." She hoped it was a safe comment.

"Generally speaking, I'm not prone to hallucinations. Therefore, I've either gone mad or what just happened was real. I prefer to think my sanity is intact, so...you do the math."

Gone was the laughing Zack, the lighthearted man who had rescued her from a fate—or a date—worse than death. Too bad because that Zack had been a lot of fun. That Zack was someone she could imagine spending time with. This one was prone to bouts of unpredictability and brooding behavior.

Maybe fun Zack was still in there.

She peered at him through her lashes and heard herself say, "Pookie bears are not very good at math."

What on earth possessed her to say that? Wasn't there supposed to be some kind of filter between her brain and her mouth? Obviously, if there was, it was not working properly. Maybe a giant flaming eagle would come through the ceiling and snatch her away but probably not.

Without giving Zack a chance to speak, Kat jumped to her feet and rushed back to the kitchen. Once there, she pulled a bottle of water from the fridge and rolled the chilled plastic against the flaming hotness of her face.

If she had taken the time to look, she would have seen the wide smile on Zack's face before the notes he was refining took over his concentration again.

Too keyed up to sleep, Kat fed one of the stacks of DVDs borrowed from Julie into her computer and added buying a player of some sort to her to-do list. As many times as she had heard her friends drool over one actor or another in a movie, it was finally her turn to see what all the fuss was about.

Ten minutes later and fully engrossed in the story, Kat chewed absently on an already frayed fingernail. When Julius cleared his throat to get her attention, she was startled enough to jump and burn him with a single glare.

He raised his hands, "Sorry." The smirk on his face completely negated the gruff apology.

Clicking pause, she turned to him and gestured for him to get on with whatever business had brought him back.

"Forgot to give you the final clue. One plus two plus three equals four." Julius nodded as he made his nonsensical pronouncement.

"Six."

"Four," Julius emphasized the word by using a firm voice and trying to communicate something more with his expression.

He had faded away before she realized he was talking about the final clue for what remained hidden in Hayward House.

CHAPTER TWELVE

Zack opened the door and ducked under the yellow crime scene tape with Kat and Amethyst hard on his heels. Kat wasn't certain how useful she would be. Psychometry, or channeling psychic information from physical items, was not her strong suit, but to put an end to this mess, she was willing to try anything.

Stepping into Logan's last known residence, Zack kept his face carefully blank, then ducked to the left side of the doorway. "Just give me your impressions as you get them. I'll stay out of your way." There wasn't time for her to try and figure out why he seemed so locked down. Kat shrugged it off and began to walk around the apartment while Amethyst stayed near the door.

Clearly, this space represented Logan before the Earthwalker had gotten hold of him. Clean lines, modern, everything in shades of white or gray. Even the art on the walls provided little in the way of contrast. A triptych of canvases hung above the fireplace, their stark whiteness broken up by a series of squares shading from palest gray to black that marched across from left to right.

The main living area was a large, open floor plan with the kitchen to the left and a great room on the right. Every piece of furniture had been chosen for visual impact over comfort. Sharp lines and angles, while interesting to look at, appeared uninviting. The entire place felt to Kat as though it was a veneer. The thin covering that disguised the lie underneath. Logan may have called this place home for a time, but he had never lived here.

She strolled toward the bedroom, lost in thoughts and impressions. Much as she had hoped to be helpful, nothing of a psychic nature was jumping out at her. Logan had not left anything of himself in any of the rooms she had seen so far.

"Are you getting anything?" Kat made her way back to where Amethyst stood.

"It's clean. Almost too clean, you know? Like his aura has been scrubbed completely away."

"Could Billy do that?"

Amethyst shrugged. The two women moved toward the bedroom.

"Once he chose a look, at least he committed. Very matchy-matchy. Could have used a pop of color."

"I know, all this white is so clinical."

"Call it a bust?" Kat asked.

"Afraid so."

Zack locked the door behind them with a vicious twist of the key.

Logic screamed that this was a colossal waste of time, while his gut insisted Kat and Amethyst would turn up a lead. For the first time ever, he was tempted to ignore his gut. Instead, he drove them to the storage facility. There was a better chance of finding something there, something personal.

Only ten city blocks separated the two locations, but the

short drive was steeped in tension, making it seem longer and unnaturally quiet. Even at his most impassive, Zack could not hide his impatience or lack of faith in her. Or, for that matter, in Amethyst. Kat burned to prove him wrong.

Pulling up to the storage facility, Kat's stomach turned over twice, then erupted into flutters of dread and excitement. She glanced over at Amethyst and saw matching misgivings. This was not going to be a repeat of what had just happened. This time they would find something.

Before Zack had time to pull to a stop, both women pointed to unit 1206.

"There."

"That one," they spoke together. Gooseflesh prickled up Zack's arms. They had chosen correctly. Unit 1206, now with its police-issued lockbox, had indeed belonged to Logan Ellis. He had already been through the contents several times and found nothing to provide a solid lead. If they found anything natural or supernatural—he cringed at the thought—he would be surprised.

The storage room door rolled up on its hinges with a screech of protest, making both women shudder. Kat immediately sensed the pervading, cold darkness that signaled the earthwalker had spent time here. Amethyst didn't have to rely on similar emotional perceptions; she could see the blackness lingering on the surface of every item like an oily cloud.

Logan had created the perfect bolthole here. A small table holding a battery-operated lamp rested beside a camp cot covered with a sleeping bag. Two plastic bins sat on the floor next to the table held an assortment of foods that could be eaten cold: granola bars, snack-sized containers of applesauce, and cans of tuna. The other was nearly empty though it had once contained a stack of forged documents: driver's licenses in various names, passports, and birth certificates. Those had all been logged into evidence leaving only a pack of matches and a length of ribbon behind; these had been considered too negligible to be of consequence.

Amethyst stepped a couple of paces into the unit and turned slowly in place. Whatever Billy the earthwalker may have done to the apartment to cleanse his aura had not been repeated here. Blackness dripped from the cot and oozed around the plastic bins. Anywhere she could see Logan's lighter colors, they were overlaid by Billy's darkness except for one spot. High up on the back wall, where the corrugated metal wall met the open raftered roof, was a flare of color that could only be Logan's alone.

She pointed, "Logan hid something there, but I can't reach it. Zack, see that tiny ledge where the wall meets the roof?"

Zack pulled a penlight from his pocket and shined it into the crevice before reaching in to pull out a coin. Roughly the size of a fifty-cent piece, it was a commemorative coin with a Santa head on one side and the name of a small theme park on the other.

"Anyone could have left this. You can't be sure it was Logan?"

"Trust me. His aura is all over it." Amethyst handed the coin to Kat, who turned it over and over in her hand before closing her fist around it. The principle of getting perceptions off of an item was not that different from reading cards or rune stones. She tuned into the coin, and by extension, into the energy Logan had poured into it.

As the images came, faintly at first, she began to speak, "He carried this in his pocket for a long time." She ignored Zack's raised eyebrow. He had dragged her here, so why was he acting skeptical?

"He was six—maybe seven—living with someone older, a man, maybe a grandfather, or foster care provider. The man was nice to him. It was the only time he ever felt safe, loved. The man never screamed at him, never hit or pinched with hard fingers, never left him to wake up alone or hungry or scared. He wanted to stay there forever."

Kat's eyes fluttered closed as she saw scene after scene unfolding in her head. The older man with kind eyes grinning at the tow-headed boy who clumsily hammered a small nail into the roof of a birdhouse. The pair paddling an aluminum canoe through perfectly still water, fishing poles, and a creel at their feet. Gentle hands teaching the boy how to tie his shoes.

"It was a perfect day. They went to a small theme park somewhere in the mountains. He fed the reindeer and rode the carousel. Ate popcorn and cotton candy. And he laughed—they laughed."

Tears streamed down her face.

"Such joy, his little heart was full. But it didn't last. Something happened. The bad man came back."

Zack started to ask a question, but she held up a hand to stop him.

"They hurt him—his parents. Used him as a pawn between them."

None of this was surprising to Zack; there were records of Logan's abusive childhood once he'd known where to look. Records that made him feel sorry for the child living in such painful circumstances, but he could not let sympathy cloud the facts of the case. Plenty of people used their abusive history as a springboard for doing good. Logan had chosen the opposite route.

When the spirit made itself known to Kat, Amethyst saw the aura but nothing more. Zack saw nothing but felt a stir in the air, a breeze no stronger than a sigh.

"He's here," Kat breathed, then opened her eyes, focused them on that nothing, and began a one-sided conversation. It gave Zack the heebie-jeebies, which surprised him after having met Estelle and Julius.

He'd faced off against a thug holding a gun and not felt as uncomfortable as he did right now. Half of him wanted to ask who was there. The other wouldn't utter that question on pain of death.

"His name is Bert. He was Logan's grandfather. Mother's side, I think."

No way had she pulled that out of thin air. He remembered the name: Bertrand Goddard.

"Bert says he took the boy in for a few months. Logan came to him hungry and covered in bruises. It took several weeks before he felt safe enough to stop hoarding food in his room. Longer still before he stopped flinching at every loud noise."

Zack watched the play of emotions across Kat's face as she relayed Bert's message.

"He's sorry for what Logan has become, sorry he didn't fight hard enough to hold on to the boy when his father came back around. Thornton laid it on thick, said he had changed his ways, and was ready to provide a better home for his son. Bert was taken in like so many others, and Logan paid the price."

More images scrolled through Kat's head. She saw Bert watching as Logan twisted in the seat to watch, one hand on the window glass, tears of utter sadness as the one person who had ever shown him true love and kindness stood and waved. Two hearts had been broken that day, and neither had ever recovered.

"Use the coin," Bert's final words to Kat echoed back as he began to fade away. "It's his touchstone."

Compassion for the boy Logan had once been and for the grandfather who had tried his best went to war with Kat's need to see the man pay for what he had done.

Justice won.

Burned.

Logan pulled the red baseball cap down to hide his face as he strolled casually past the storage unit. Somehow the cop from that podunk little town had tracked him here. Everything in the unit was burned. Even the…he tried not to think about the loss of the one item he had carried with him all these years. It was gone now, along with everything else.

With Billy pulled back, for the time being, there was enough Logan left to mourn the loss of an item so important he had carried it with him for twenty years. The last remnants of the little boy were not strong enough to influence regret in the grown man for the things he had done, but then, he had stopped lamenting the loss of his innocence a long, long time ago.

The boy who left his grandfather's house that day had shattered to leave his soul in pieces behind the car like a trail of breadcrumbs he would never follow home.

Those days of safety, the last of his childhood, would go from being cherished memories to being the impetus for a belief that he deserved everything, whether he had earned it or not. Someone had done the earning, and that was a good enough excuse for taking whatever he could and never counting the cost.

After all, Logan had been trained by the best. Even in his tender youth, he knew Thornton was piling it on thick with his story of how he had changed, how he had a safe place to live, and money for food.

None of it was true, and the little boy could not understand how his grandfather had been deceived. To his mind, the old man had betrayed him. Whether Bert had no legal standing to force Thornton's hand didn't matter. He had let Logan go without a fight.

Before that year was out, Thornton had trained his son, by

liberal use of the flat of his hand, to be the perfect shill. First, with easy things like selling religious booklets to farmers' wives, then moving up to selling higher ticket items to the farmers themselves. Their most lucrative con had been taking half the down payment on a new tractor and disappearing with the money.

Logan knew what he was doing was wrong, that Burt would not approve—and whatever had twisted in his mind made Burt's displeasure into his biggest motivation to succeed. Logan never understood that his biggest con was when he deluded himself into thinking he was making Burt pay for abandoning him to this life.

Zack saw the sorrow in her eyes, but without the visual replay of history, he only knew the details from the outside. To him, this man who had hurt his sister and tried to hurt Kat was not worth her tears. Her compassion for the slimeball got under his skin.

So what if Ellis had a rough childhood? He wasn't the only one. Plenty of kids survived abuse to grow up productive citizens. If Ellis was one of the exceptions, he had chosen to be.

Bleeding hearts never wanted criminals punished for their crimes, and while Zack knew everyone had the potential for rehabilitation, it never came without some type of a wake-up call followed by a personal decision. He doubted Logan Ellis had the guts for that kind of change.

CHAPTER THIRTEEN

When Zack offered to drive Kat home, Amethyst, standing out of sight, shot her an exaggerated eyebrow waggle that was returned by a glare that, if looks really could kill, would have leveled a city block. Kat never even got a chance to weigh in before Amethyst suddenly remembered a pressing errand that would take her in the opposite direction and be so incredibly boring that Kat would be much better off accepting Zack's kind offer. The next thing she knew, it was a done deal.

"Subtle," Kat observed dryly as she watched her friend walk away so quickly you'd think her shoes were on fire. Then she grinned at Zack, "You up for a visit with Kane and Molly? My treat as a thank you for the ride."

"I keep telling Molly there must be something illegal in that meatloaf because it's habit-forming. You could opt for the Guinea pig special if you're feeling adventurous."

"Tell me it's not really Guinea pig." Kat shuddered at the thought.

"What? No, it's whatever dish they're experimenting with that day, but you're not allowed to ask what's in it before you order."

"Sounds like a crapshoot. What's their track record like?"

"Pretty good. There was lobster aspic that went way wrong once. Ended up looking like Jabba the Hutt and tasted like feet, but mostly Kane does okay. He's the one who comes up with the recipes, and then Molly handles the daily menus and runs the kitchen. They make a good team."

"Jabba the Hutt, a visual reference I can actually remember."

"Star Wars fan?"

"I was a sci-fi geek before I lost my sight. Some movies you can listen to and get a good idea of what's happening, but a good space epic is so visual that I limited my exposure to reading only." No self-pity, just the bare facts.

"Favorite book?"

"Ender's Game. No question."

"You know they made it into a movie, right?"

"I'd heard, and it's on my list of ones I'm sad not to have seen at the cinema. It won't be the same on my teeny tiny television set."

"What if I told you I have a copy of the movie *with* extra features and a seventy-inch flat screen?"

"I guess I'd say 'beam me up.'"

"Wrong franchise. And speaking of—you'll need to watch the new Star Treks and then the Marvel movies, and then there's…I'll make you a list." He felt the faintest flutter of nerves as he asked, "So we'll have Molly cook us up some food and then hit my place for the movie?"

For a second, he was afraid she might say yes to the food, no to the movie. It surprised him how much he was already looking forward to sharing the experience with her, at how he could feel so comfortable around her while there was still that heart-pumping, stomach-jumping feeling of attraction running deeper than any he'd known before.

The woman had guts, no question. He admired that about her. She also had skin that looked soft as the petals on a daisy and those eyes—every time they turned his way, it was like falling off a cliff.

On the other side of the car, Kat's thoughts ran along similar lines. Zack was the perfect combination of safe and dangerous. Every accidental touch sent waves of delicious electricity tingling through her. It was that same feeling she'd had on her first roller coaster ride in the days before her life had turned into one.

Sitting next to her cousin, Sue, and screaming with laughter and fear, they had learned dread during the long climb, then plunged down that first hill and got a taste of how it felt to have adrenaline coursing through their veins. Heady stuff, not unlike sitting next to Zack in a car small enough to have his arm brushing against hers at every turn.

Her face flamed red as she let herself think about what the full ride with him might be like. Maybe tonight, she would finally let herself find out. Virginity at her age was more of an embarrassment than a virtue. At this point, she was torn between waiting for the right man and just getting it over with.

Zack looked like the type of guy who could help her out on that score. But what if he didn't think of her that way? What if she was nothing more than his sister's friend, and this was a pity movie? She chided herself for letting her thoughts stray down that particular path.

Kat's shoulders hunched as though expecting a blow as she tried with a sideways look to figure out what he might be thinking. The look on his face was open, friendly, and hard to gauge.

She was still trying to parse out his level of emotion when he pulled into the tiny lot behind the pub. Before he could make his way around the car to open her door, she'd already scrambled out, so he hit the locks, swung the door shut with a thunk, then reached for her hand as they walked toward the rear entrance.

The contact did nothing to quiet her chaotic thoughts.

"You've gone quiet," he stated in a low voice, "second thoughts?"

"No, just things on my mind." If he only knew.

An hour later, she was sliding back into his car with a smile on her face and a belly full of good food. She'd gone with the delectably flaky beer-battered fish this time.

"An extra hour of running tomorrow but totally worth it."

Molly's teasing had lightened Kat's mood. When Zack pulled up next to a narrow, two-storied brick building that should have been flanked by others of its kind but now stood alone, the last remaining relic of Brinford's town center.

"What's this place?" She leaned across to get a better look.

"Home. Come see."

He unlocked the thick security door set into the left side of the front of the building and led her into what had once been Brinford Bank. It hadn't changed all that much in the intervening years.

Nearly twice as deep as it was wide, the whole place had a definite hallway feel because the interior was divided neatly in half. The former customer area on the left boasted a high ceiling that arched up two full stories. The business side on the right featured a loft area where the main offices had been located. Below that was the counter area where the tellers once counted money.

That area had been turned into a galley kitchen. Some clever artisan figured out a way to incorporate the barred teller windows into the cabinet fronts to maintain the feel of the original space.

Glancing up, Kat saw the glass fronts where the offices had

been but could not tell what use Zack was making of those rooms from where she stood.

The front lobby area was now his main living space. The huge flat-screen television he had told her about hung between heavily curtained windows. It faced a long sectional sofa set that looked inviting and was currently home to a fat black cat who appeared bored but whose green eyes never left the new guest in the room.

"Wow." Kat moved farther into the room to take a closer look and noticed the gleaming vault door at the end of the room. "May I?" He waved her ahead, and she stepped to the doorway to peek inside.

Most of the vault interior consisted of safety deposit doors and shelves, all in a dull brass finish. The only furniture in the room was the bed. For everything else, he had cleverly converted what was already there. He'd pulled out and braced safety deposit boxes, drilled holes into the sides, and used them to hold clothes bars as a makeshift closet.

Beside the bed, more drawers were braced into place and topped with simple planks to create bedside tables. Another set of them formed a bench softened with a brightly patterned cushion.

It was a unique setup and oddly homey, but the two large-scale canvases on either side of the windows in his living space made Kat suck in a breath. Painted with precise, slashing strokes, the paintings completed a gritty urban diptych that immediately made her feel the city's energy.

The artist captured the skyline against lowering storm clouds with great detail. One spear of sunlight broke through to illuminate a small figure in the foreground, a little boy shown from the back dangling a teddy bear in one tiny hand. She didn't need to see his face to know he was alone and scared; it was all there in the set of his shoulders, the tilt of his head.

Powerful and emotional.

She looked at the signature and then turned to him with a stunned expression. "You?"

He nodded. "It's a hobby."

"A hobby? With talent like this?"

"The second evil."

"Do they know you can paint like this?"

"They do." Zack changed the subject. "Ready for that movie?"

Kat relaxed on the sofa and idly reached out to pet the great lump of black fur. The cat rewarded her with a mighty yawn before sliding onto her lap, settling in for a loud purr. "Bring it, geek boy."

"That's geek man to you."

"Nice uniform." She took in his snug jeans and the navy sweater that played nicely off his brown eyes and got a smirk in exchange as he settled beside her. Close.

Close enough that his thigh brushed against hers and sent that shocking tingle up her spine.

Then the movie started, and she quickly became so engrossed in the action she almost forgot he was there. Tuning out the world while reading or watching a good movie was a skill she remembered from before.

Yet, she knew the moment Zack's warm hand closed over her own, felt each delicious movement as he turned her hand in his to thread his fingers with hers, enjoyed the fluttering low in her belly as he stroked his thumb absently across her skin.

If he could make her feel like this with a simple touch, what would it feel like to kiss him? She snuggled closer and hoped to find out.

When he felt her settle closer, Zack lost track of the film and turned all his attention to Kat. Shifting slightly, he let go of the hand he was holding and slid an arm around her instead. Sensing he was in the way, the cat slithered to the floor to find another comfortable spot.

Zack flexed his arm to pull her closer; he had to know, to taste.

And his phone shrilled out the tone that signaled an emergency.

Half tempted to ignore it, he swore and levered himself off the sofa. Grabbing the phone, he punched the answer button with savage force.

"Roman." He barked and heard the wince on the other end as the dispatcher, a very nice young woman named Dannisha, spoke excitedly into his ear, "Sir, there's a disturbance at your sister's house. Her alarm system was triggered. I've already sent a car, but I knew you would want to know."

"Thanks, Danni." He clicked off the phone just as Estelle shivered into view.

"It's Logan. Finn and the little girl are with her. Julius stayed behind to keep watch. Hurry."

By the time Zack had retrieved his service weapon, Kat was already waiting for him at the door, and the pair of them, interlude forgotten, raced to check on Gustavia.

The silence during the short ride was made of worry and rose up like a miasma between them.

"...do the right thing. I know it's in you. Where's that little boy I knew who had such sweetness, such heart...do the right thing..." Even though he knew Logan's heart was probably closed to him forever, Bert continued his litany. But if there were a chance, no matter how slim that his words would sink in and find purchase on some shard of decency, no matter how deeply that shard might be buried, he would keep whispering into the boy's ear.

111

Do the right thing. Do the right thing.

Logan didn't know where the words were coming from, only that they kept repeating through his mind like a hammer on a nail. Endlessly sinking, piercing through until they touched the last vestige of humanity left to him by Billy or by Thornton. The vision of him beating Gustavia, throwing her into the back of a car, played across his memory.

Do the right thing. Do the right thing.

He'd felt the devil inside him already. Was this the angel come to sit on his shoulder now?

Do the right thing.

Without knowing the outcome, Bert relentlessly drove Logan back to Oakville until he ended up in the very last place he should ever have gone. Gustavia's front step.

Finn's daughter, Samantha, was already asleep in Gustavia's spare room when Fritzie went on full alert. Ears back, he dashed toward the front door just as a heavy thud shook it in its frame.

Chaos erupted as the house alarm shot to life with a blare, followed by Sam's piercing shriek. "Daddy…"

"Go to Sam," Gustavia gave Finn a shove as she snatched up Fritzie with shaking hands and keyed in the code to shut the alarm down.

In the blessed silence that followed, her ears rang for a moment, and then she heard it. The faint sound of crying coming from outside.

Finn strode into the room, cradling his daughter, her eyes wide with fear. He was just in time to see Gustavia yank open the front door and peer into the night.

"What do you think you're doing? Get back in here." He moved to pull her away from nearly certain danger, but she shrugged him off. Just at the edge of the shadows cast by the

112

motion sensor spotlight mounted above the door, she could see a dark form.

"Shh. Listen."

Then Finn heard it, too. A ragged voice repeated, "Help me. Please, I'm sorry. The right thing."

Sirens rang out in the distance, and the shadow slid deeper into the night. Gustavia knew he would be long gone before the first flare of red and blue reached the house.

She was still standing in the open doorway when Zack pulled up in front and parked illegally. Even with the excitement coursing through her veins, Gustavia quirked an eyebrow at her brother as Kat stepped out of the car. Angrily, he brushed off her quizzical look and demanded to know why she wasn't still locked inside the house where she belonged.

"He wasn't trying to hurt me. It wasn't Billy. It was Logan out here crying for help."

"I don't care if he was bringing you the Hope diamond," Zack punctuated each word by poking her in the shoulder and taking a step forward to drive her back indoors, "you stay inside the house."

"She's right, son," Julius spoke from just behind him startled Zack. "And so is he," the ghost wagged a finger at Gustavia.

Turning on his heel, Zack stalked back outside, slamming the door behind him, and joined his deputy in what he knew was a futile search through the neighborhood. His gut had already told him the danger was minimal, and it was already too late. Logan would be well out of reach. It was why he hadn't bothered calling in for extra backup, but none of it made up for Gustavia's foolish behavior.

The early spring mix of melting snow and emerging mud crept into Zack's running shoes like frigid slugs, but he kept walking until it cooled his temper enough to go back and take his sister's statement.

"For the fifth time, we heard a thud. The alarm went off. Finn took care of Sam while I turned off the alarm, and that's when I heard him crying outside. I opened the door. He saw me and pleaded for help, then ran off. That's it. There's nothing more to remember."

Julius chimed in to say he was certain it had been Logan and not Billy outside Gustavia's door. Estelle returned from a quick trip to Hayward House to report there had been no disturbance there.

"I don't understand why he would come to me of all people and ask for help. I didn't like him before he turned into some kind of skin Muppet."

"Don't you mean puppet?" Kat asked, knowing Gustavia probably had some logical reason for her word choice. Gustavia logic.

"Hey, you watched what you watched when you were a kid, and I watched what I watched. No judging."

CHAPTER FOURTEEN

Bottles was surprisingly clean and well-kept for a dimly lit neighborhood bar. Two competition-sized pool tables took up space in the quieter back section of the building, while the front area held booths and a handful of four-tops that filled up fast on live karaoke night.

This was where Tyler found Zack, and to his surprise, it was where he also found Julius.

Man and ghost were embroiled in a heated discussion over a set of notes on the table. Tyler watched with interest as Zack saw him coming and surreptitiously slid some of those notes off the table and out of sight.

"It won't work. We had a perfectly good plan. Why have you changed it?" Julius nodded to Tyler and continued to insist on an answer.

"Of course, it will. I've done my research on Ellis. This is exactly the type of thing a cheap con man like him will fall for. He won't be able to resist."

"And how much research have you done on Billy the Earthwalker?"

Zack's features twisted as he snorted in derision, "Earthwalker."

Pointing to himself, Julius said, "Ghost," the Captain Obvious was implied.

Sliding into the booth next to Julius and pulling the notebook over for a quick glance, Tyler jumped into the conversation, "He's right, Zack. If it were just Logan we were dealing with, your approach would be foolproof. Billy's more than a complication, and until we have a better idea what motivates him, there's no way to predict his end game."

"Ellis showed up at her place last night, and now I'm not good with using my sister as bait. Sorry if that throws a crimp in Caspar's plan, but it's not going to happen."

Julius puffed up and prepared to square off against Zack, who, it appeared, had no intention of giving so much as an inch. Tyler had just prepared himself to play referee when Finn and Reid walked in together.

Having had the longest association with the group of women involved, Tyler knew perfectly well they would do whatever they thought was necessary, whether anyone liked it or not. But he understood Zack's desire to protect Gustavia since he felt the same way about Julie.

Finn slid in next to Zack while Reid snagged a chair from a nearby empty table and made himself comfortable at the end of the booth. After the greetings were dispensed with, Tyler flashed a pointed look at Zack, then turned to Julius, "I'd like to hear your plan."

First, Julius reviewed how he had let Billy into the world while Tyler made notes on a newly acquired tablet device. Then, he asked Tyler for a brief summary of events to date.

As Tyler spoke, Zack's expression darkened. He'd been kept out of the loop for months now, and on top of that, every single one of them had suppressed evidence that might have led him to Logan's capture long before.

When it was over, he lurched to his feet and slammed his hand on the table for emphasis, "I could arrest every single one of you on obstruction charges. What did you think you were playing at?"

Struggling to keep an amused smile off his face and maintain a mild, even tone in the face of Zack's mood, Finn simply asked, "And would you have believed us if we had told you everything?"

"Probably not," Zack continued to bluster, "but I had a right to know when it was my sister in danger."

"Sit down, young man." Julius' command brooked no refusal. "You all have a common enemy. Let that be enough to bind you. Time is short, and my energy is limited, so if you don't mind, let's get on with it, and you can save your recriminations for later."

Still glowering, Zack relented and took his seat.

"The way I see it," Reid finally spoke, "is that Billy wants to live again, and the way to do that is to gain complete control over Logan's body. To do so, he must either blacken or weaken Logan's soul, so he has complete control or kill it entirely, but he is unsure if the latter would kill the body as well." He looked to Julius for a nod of confirmation.

"Let's say I drank the Kool-Aid and believe all this…" Zack couldn't come up with a suitable word to describe the theory, so he just circled a finger at his temple, "why is he still gunning for my sister and Julie? Stupid to keep going after them than to hole up somewhere and do his dirty work in private."

It was a good question.

"Galmadriel thinks Billy uses Logan's anger as his anchor to the body. What happened last night says his control is nowhere near as complete as we thought. Logan managed to slip it long enough to beg for forgiveness. Billy will need to pull off

117

something big to make up for that, and she guesses that he won't wait long."

"I'd feel sorry for the man if it wasn't my woman he was after," Finn nearly growled the words.

"Right then, what does Galmadriel suggest? Something to do with the second set of notes Zack's hiding?"

"It's not going to happen. She wants to use Julie and Gustavia as bait," Zack insisted.

Julius shot Zack a raised eyebrow. "No, Julie and Gustavia will not be bait. They will be the trap. Here's how it will play out…"

While Julius laid it out for the men, Estelle gathered the four women to prepare them for a planning session with Galmadriel.

"Whatever you do, don't argue with her," Amethyst advised. She'd been in the room with the angel when Julius had tried it and still remembered the feeling of being choked by energy.

Kat had no intention of arguing. As fear ran through her like water, she doubted she could squeak out a single word in the presence of an angel. Her grandmother, the one who laid out the cards and talked to the dead, had also prayed over the bread those activities put on the table. Granted, Madame Zephyr's view on heaven didn't exactly track along the same path that her church-going friends followed, but she was devout in her beliefs and had passed those along to Kat.

Amethyst must have seen something of that fear in the colors of Kat's aura because she reached out with her healing touch to pluck away some of the tension. Kat closed her eyes; there were still times when she felt safest in the dark.

"I am here." Amethyst had described the angel's voice as sounding like a trumpet but with a bell-like quality, but Kat was still unprepared for the deep vibration and ringing

118

resonance of Galmadriel's speech. Or for the volume.

"Tone it down some." Hearing Estelle caution the angel was what pried Kat's eyes open just the tiniest bit. "You're shaking the chandelier."

When the angel responded with an apology at a much lower, gentler volume, Kat couldn't resist and took a glance. At first, all she saw was light surrounding a vague figure. Dazzled by the brilliance, Kat could not make out any distinguishing features before squeezing her eyes closed again. The brightness was just too much for her.

Galmadriel noticed, and abruptly, the glare reduced to a bearable level. Directly into Kat's mind, she said, "You may open them now. I forgot to adjust. It will not happen again. You have my word."

Such a feeling of well-being washed over Kat that she had little choice but to obey. Without the light and sound show, Galmadriel looked almost ordinary at first.

Wavy auburn hair fell to the angel's shoulders and framed a heart-shaped face with pale blue eyes under gently arched brows in that same pretty color. She looked like a soccer mom. Early thirties, russet-colored sweater over brown slacks. You could walk right past her on the street without a second thought.

But, when Kat glanced away to gauge her friend's reactions and then looked back, the angel's appearance was completely different. She was now a brunette, a decade older, with brown eyes above wide cheekbones and a slightly squared jaw.

Fascinated, Kat blinked slowly, and when she opened her eyes again, she saw a teenager with jet-black hair, a pierced lip, and kitted out in full Goth-style clothing and makeup.

The only thing that remained unchanged was the angel's voice.

Three rapid blinks and three new versions later, Kat

wondered if she could blink one eye and then the other and catch the change as it happened when she realized the others were already discussing Logan.

"…still hope for him," Estelle was saying, "if we save brute force as a last result and work with whatever humanity he has left."

Galmadriel focused on Gustavia to ask, "Will you be able to put vengeance aside after your previous experience with this man?"

Gustavia opened her mouth to answer, then snapped it shut again while she gave the question the serious consideration it deserved. "Honestly, Logan doesn't deserve my forgiveness, but he will have it anyway because I don't want to carry that much negativity around."

"That will do." Galmadriel's gaze next rested on Julie. "And you—will you also be capable of forgiveness?"

"I believe I can. What he did was horrible, but what Billy has done to him is worse."

The angel nodded, then morphed into a child with blond hair in ringlets, dressed in a pinafore. Kat shivered when the girl opened her mouth and spoke in that resonant, adult-sounding voice. "During his lifetime, the earthwalker believed the division between masculine and feminine was indicative of intelligence and ability."

"Nice way of saying he was a misogynist. Very PC." Amethyst approved.

"PC?"

"Politically Correct." Julie supplied the definition.

Galmadriel, now looking as she had during each encounter with Amethyst, shrugged and continued, "If everything goes according to plan, those traits Billy considered weak and beneath him will be his downfall."

Then, with no more changing of bodies and an economy of

words, the angel laid it out for them.

It started with Julius using his tenuous connection with Billy to goad the earthwalker back to prominence.

The plan was a little dangerous, a little daring, and more than a little elegant in its simplicity.

Kat knew the men would hate it, but it would work.

Now all they had to do was wait.

Before Galmadriel took her leave, Kat worked up the courage to speak.

"Galmadriel, may I ask you a question?" Her voice quavered at the end as Kat twisted her hands in her lap, hoping she wasn't way out of line.

"You may."

"Is there a way to...?" Not sure how to frame the question without hurting Estelle's feelings, Kat swallowed hard, then continued, "I see spirits everywhere," she ended lamely.

"That is a statement, not a question. Are you asking if there is a way to retain a certain amount of privacy when needed?"

Relieved, Kat chanced a sidelong look at Estelle, then nodded.

"That's exactly it. No offense Estelle, but they're everywhere. I never get a moment's peace; sometimes, they tell me inappropriate things about the people in the room. I know they mean well, but sometimes I just want to be left alone." The words fell from her lips in a rush.

"None taken," Estelle assured.

"Close your eyes." Galmadriel reached out and, with a touch, showed Kat how to erect a simple barrier that filtered out most spirit energy. Speaking directly into Kat's mind, she explained, "This will not work on Estelle or Julius. Since you have channeled them, they can now vibrate within your unique frequency, but I believe they will respect the boundary."

Galmadriel withdrew her presence to let Kat try on her own. A flexing of intention and the barrier shimmered into place as easily as blinking.

"Thank you. I promise I will only use it when absolutely necessary."

"To everything a balance." Was that humor in the angel's eyes? Kat thought so.

"I will return when I am needed. Until then, be watchful."

Kat's ears popped with the changing pressure from Galmadriel's departure. Then, her voice echoed in the room, "Do not forget the key."

"The key?"

"Equinox is getting closer. We should plan a get-together this weekend to see if we can find the last key."

CHAPTER FIFTEEN

With all eight of them crowded in front of the spring-themed stained glass window, Julie could not help but take a moment to reflect on the journey that had brought this group together.

She saw herself a year ago standing here alone, worried about the future of Hayward House, and wished she could tell that lonely, scared woman from the past to keep the faith. Things would change for the better.

She watched Zack step forward to scan the window looking for anything that might help them locate the final key. Since the math clue Julius had given Kat made no sense to anyone yet, they decided to start with the magic garden, spring-style.

Julie smiled at Tyler as he sat poised with his laptop, ready to note their findings on one of his famous lists. No matter what they turned up this time, she already had all the treasure she needed—a loving husband, a home no longer in grave need of repair, a group of friends who made up her new family, and a few extra months with her beloved Grams.

Like the other windows, its centerpiece was a large tree depicted in spring's lighter, fresher greens. Below the tree, a carpet of new grass studded with abstract flowers was rendered with intricately cut glass in bright Easter egg colors that provided a visual balance and counterpoint to the pale blues and whites of a gently clouded sky.

While they watched, Gustavia sidled up to Julie and whispered, "Look at them. Do you see it? Chemistry."

"Oh, I see it." It was nothing overt, more like an extra bit of awareness between them, but it was hard to miss if you were looking.

"And how does that make you feel?" Julie tried to imitate Freud, but her fake German accent was so bad it came out sounding more like French."

With a giggle, Gustavia replied, "Well, Sigmund, it makes me feel all fluttery inside. And like, maybe, we could give them a little nudge."

Gustavia met Julie's grin with an exaggerated eyebrow waggle and raised her voice to ask, "Find anything?"

"Yes," Kat glanced over her shoulder. "We've either found a set of red herrings or multiple possibilities."

Intrigued, the other six crowded even closer while Kat showed them. "There's a set of pins the same as the ones that held the painting of Julius on the first window." She lifted her chin toward him, and Zack swung them into place.

"Here, here, here, here, and here," she pointed out, "I've found the same types of ledges that held those lenses from the second window. And then there are three spots where the leading feels exactly like the sections with the hidden prism brackets—the same as the ones on the winter window."

"Do you think we need to find a new set of keys or use the

ones from before?"

"*One plus two plus three equals four.* I think Julius meant for us to use those keys again. That would fit with his math clue."

It felt right, and Julie figured that if they were wrong, Julius would hound them until they looked deeper.

CHAPTER SIXTEEN

If Gustavia had been here, she would have told him to trust the universe. He didn't know if he believed in fate, but the fact that he had walked into another of Kat's unfortunate dates was a coincidence even he could not ignore.

He could tell she didn't want to be there by her body language. Elbow on the table, shoulders slumped, her cheek resting on her hand, and her eyes were glazed over with boredom while the man across from her droned on.

It was his civic duty to rescue her yet again. Protect and serve. So what if neither of those quite described the current situation?

Zack knew the moment she noticed him standing there. It was evident in the delicate tension that ran through her body. He hoped for more, but her only response was a wry twist of the lips and the slightest hint of an eyeball roll.

Unable to resist, Zack made his way to the table. Completely ignoring the man sitting on the other side, he leaned down, grasped Kat's arm gently, and hissed just loud enough for her date to hear, "There's not much time. Follow me." He glanced behind him as though looking for someone who might be tailing him.

Kat wasted no time jumping into character. She darted a glance left, then right, and pasted a frightened look on her face as she let him gently drag her to her feet.

With only an apologetic shrug to her erstwhile date, Kat grabbed her coat and purse from the back of the chair and left the restaurant.

"Come with me if you want to live," Zack pulled her along gently but forcefully.

"Really?" Now she was getting worried. Had something happened?

"No." Once outside and around the corner, he stopped to grin down at her, "I just always wanted to say that." Before he could help himself, he bent down and pressed his lips to hers.

Kat trembled before the onslaught of desire overtook her, and she kissed him back. What had started soft and sweet very quickly turned passionate as she wound her arms around his neck and pressed her body to his. He was like molten lava running through her veins, igniting fires in places she never knew existed. Fires that threatened to burn out of control.

A split second of surprise at her response flitted through his mind before he abandoned rational thought, gathered her closer, then closer still, and poured the whole of himself into the kiss.

Sparks of electricity raced across her skin, arrowed into her gut until there was no escaping the need. She wanted—well, she didn't know what exactly but knew it was something only he could give her. "Please," she whispered.

Thinking she was asking him to stop, he began to pull back slowly from the kiss.

He only realized he was wrong, that she wanted more when she pulled his head back down. Then all rational thought fled as he plundered her lips, tasted the unbearable sweetness that was hers alone, and slid his hands down her back to pull her ever closer.

Breath mingling with breath, the sweet tension mounted until Kat pulled back, opened her eyes, and rested her forehead against his to let her racing heart slow back to normal. When she felt in control again, she trapped his face between her hands and let her eyes rove over his features, drinking them in.

"There you are," she breathed. "Just look at you." If she never saw another thing, to take that face with her into the darkness would have been enough.

Finally satisfied that she had committed every line and plane, every texture of his skin to memory, with a last caress, Kat let her hands slide away and down to take his hand in hers. She led him the short distance back to her house.

Willingly, Zack followed. There was no other choice; he was too drunk with her presence to do otherwise. She unlocked the door and pulled him inside.

As soon as the door closed, his control slipped. Brushing her coat away with an impatient motion, Zack bent his head and fitted his lips to hers. Kiss after drugging kiss. She returned them all.

Hearts pounding, breath coming faster, he whispered, "your bedroom, where is it?"

"Upstairs," she murmured against his lips, "But you should know…I've never…"

Her words hit him like a blast of cold water.

"What?"

Kat repeated, confused by the sudden change, "I've never…you know."

"Never?" He released her abruptly and dragged a hand through his hair. He was mortified at how he had been kissing her and his lack of control. This was not the way her first time should play out. If he had known, he would have acted differently, held the reins tighter.

She took his self-censure for lack of interest, and instead of being hurt by it, she got mad. "Sorrrrry," she drawled, "I had no idea my lack of experience would be such a turn-off."

He just stared at her, dumbfounded, then shook his head. What was happening here? Parts of his body were still on high alert, and those parts also had not completely relinquished control of his brain. Turn off? Not hardly.

"I never said that. I didn't mean you misunderstood."

"Misunderstood what? That you draw the line at deflowering virgins? Get out." She swung past him to wrench open the door and, when he didn't move fast enough, repeated, "Get out. Now."

The next thing he knew, the door practically slammed on his heels. Zack stood on her front step for a moment to gather his thoughts. In just a few minutes, he'd gone from being on top of the world to so low he would have to look up to see an ant's belly button.

The whole situation was ridiculous. The smart thing to do would be to walk away.

Instead, he knocked on the door.

She must have been standing right on the other side because she pulled it open immediately. Just look at her, he thought as she stood, blocking the door with scorn in her eyes. She's beautiful.

"What?" Kat prompted when he stood staring.

Rational thought gone, he opened his mouth and, instead of an eloquent apology, blurted out, "I just wanted to tell you it doesn't matter. I don't mind if you're inexperienced."

Her eyes widened, then narrowed into twin lasers that pinned him in place. "Well, that's mighty big of you, Zack. I appreciate that you are willing to lower your standards."

The door slammed again, and this time he had the sense to walk away before he made things any worse. If he wasn't careful, he might call her fat or something.

CHAPTER SEVENTEEN

If there was anything to make a woman feel like a teenager again, it was the driver's exam. Kat's knees felt like jelly, which was probably what had attracted the butterflies currently practicing flight patterns just below her sternum.

"Tell me why I want to do this again." She ordered Gustavia, who had volunteered to drive her to the county courthouse where the test was being held.

"It's a rite of passage, and you have to do it. You know you want to. It's an hour, max. You'll do fine. If you get nervous, you can imagine the instructor in his underwear."

"What? Why would I do that?" And now she wouldn't be able to do anything else. "Is that really a thing?"

"It's the accepted method for calming stage fright. Evens the playing field."

"This. Is. Not. Helping."

"But the butterflies are gone, right?" Gustavia smirked.

"Yes. Satisfied?" Kat grinned and relaxed. She had this.

That optimism stayed with her until the instructor opened the door and settled into the passenger seat. Then the butterflies returned, and judging by the buzzing in her ears, they had been joined by bees. Thousands of bees.

"So this is what you do in your spare time? Administer driving exams?" Kat asked dryly as Zack buckled his seatbelt.

"Joe has the flu. I offered to stand in." Trying to keep the conversation on track, he directed her to pull away from the curb. Mid-day, during the time of year when tourists found warmer places to be meant the only other car on the street was a minivan. Kat pulled out behind it and followed along until Zack asked her to turn right while he scribbled something on his clipboard.

The desire to say something personal came off him in waves that washed over her, but whatever was on his mind, it was nothing she wanted to hear.

After all the buildup, the driving test was fairly simple, a pass-through town, then loop back and run through a series of cones in the municipal parking lot. Despite everything, Kat performed flawlessly. Even the dreaded parallel parking was a cinch, thanks to Gustavia's generosity in taking her out every day for a week's worth of lessons.

Throughout the ordeal, she maintained cool civility, forcing Zack to respond in kind. He handed her a temporary license, paused on the verge of speaking again, and then exited the car when she snatched it from him with a perfunctory and dismissive "Thank you."

Climbing back into the car, Gustavia thought the temperature had dropped several degrees. Something had happened between Zack and Kat, and she was determined to figure out what.

"This calls for a celebration night. Wait, you passed, right? Hard to tell with that mopey expression on your face."

Given a choice between retail therapy and live karaoke, Kat chose to play and sing. Shopping still wasn't high on her list of fun things to do. The sheer number of colors and styles provided too much visual stimulation. After a short time, she felt overwhelmed and panicky. Some things would take time to get used to.

Feeling like a child raiding her mother's makeup drawer, Kat surveyed the one thing she had enjoyed shopping for, a huge supply of cosmetics. Browsing a whole series of YouTube videos made everything look easy, so she let herself indulge. Pots and tubes, sticks and compacts full of color ranged across the table.

So many choices.

Most items looked familiar, but the packaging had changed a lot. The last time she applied anything to her face besides moisturizer, she had been fourteen years old and needed little more than lip gloss, a faint touch of blusher, and a bit of mascara to look fresh and young. This was a whole new experience.

Basics. The video said to begin with some type of foundation, so she chose one in powder form. The label said it contained minerals and would give her face a flawless finish. We'll see about that, she thought, as she used a fluffy brush to smooth it on, then followed with a light dusting of blusher.

Kat angled her face to look at first one side, then the other.

Not bad.

Eyes next. A simple, smoky eye. According to the video, that would be easy and foolproof.

The first step dark eyeliner. Following the demonstration, she picked up a tube in a shade of deep gray, almost black liquid form, and twisted it open. The supplied brush looked very similar to the one in the video, so she tentatively touched it to her outer lash line.

It tickled, and she blinked without thinking and turned what was supposed to be a well-defined line into a huge smudge. Clearly, applying makeup was harder than it looked. She snatched up a cleansing wipe, cleaned away the mess, and then reapplied the base.

This time she was prepared for the tickle but not for how easy it was to slip and poke the tiny brush into her eye. Black tears dripped down one cheek as she squinted until the pain subsided.

With a growl of frustration, Kat felt like flinging the tube of eyeliner across the room but settled for giving it a shake instead. Who needed black rings around their eyes anyway?

More wiping, more foundation, and this time, she selected a pencil type of eyeliner. That liquid stuff was way too hard to control.

The pencil went on much easier, even if the line was a little more blurred. Close enough. She did the other eye and surveyed the results.

Better.

A sweep of slate gray shadow followed by a hint of sparkling silver on the inside corner, and she had to admit her eyes looked dramatic. The darkness on her lids brought out their color and made them seem more deeply blue, if that was possible.

Twisting open the cap, she pulled the mascara brush from the tube and breathed in the sharp smell. At least that hadn't changed in all these years, though the brush looked completely different from the fuzzy tip she remembered.

Surprised how quickly her hands fell back into the appropriate motions, Kat applied a light coat to her lashes and tried not to blink until it dried. She smiled at the heavy, sticky feeling, then smoothed on a pretty, pink lip gloss before opening her closet to pick out some clothes.

After so many years of seeing shades of black and gray,

Kat's eye was drawn unerringly to the brightest colors in her wardrobe, and she settled on a simple but fitted sweater in a bright, electric blue over jeans. Perfect.

She was just about to yank it over her head when it occurred to her that she might smudge the makeup she had just painstakingly applied. Making a mental note to remember the proper order of things next time, Kat eased into the sweater with minimal damage.

This fussing with appearances took up a lot more time than she had expected. Used to throwing on whatever she grabbed out of the closet, checking the buttons and beads to make sure the colors went together, but never seeing how she looked had been liberating in some ways. It wasn't as though she had gone out looking like a slob or anything, but it was a huge difference compared to this new habit of staring in the mirror.

Surveying herself for one final time, she decided that a new cut and maybe some styling lessons were in order, but all in all, even with all the extra time, she had enjoyed the experience. Something about it left her feeling more womanly, more sophisticated. A final spritz of perfume and Kat was out the door, flying down the stairs feeling lighter than she had in years.

Ten minutes late, Amethyst pulled up in front of Kat's house and prepared to go inside. Kat bounced out of the house, down the steps to yank open the passenger side door and slide into the battered, red Honda.

Seeing the exuberance of movement, such a change from the slow and careful steps in the past, brought a lump to Amethyst's throat. She swallowed hard around it while a fierce grin lit her face. Tonight, they would celebrate for more than one reason.

"Do I look okay?" Kat asked, "It's the first time I've put on makeup in years."

"You did fine. Better than fine, really. I usually poke myself in the eye with my mascara brush."

"Liquid eyeliner." Kat's laugh rang out, and Amethyst cast a sidelong glance at her aura; it was lighter than before, with flickers of yellow. "That stuff is just plain evil, and it tickles."

"Are you getting overwhelmed with all these new experiences? You know you don't have to try and make up for lost time all at once."

"I know, but it feels like I've been in a time warp and might never catch up." Kat's hands twisted nervously, but Amethyst could tell she wasn't even aware it was happening. Taking one hand off the wheel, she reached over to still their hectic motion and to soothe. "Then you turn to your friends and your family. You talk it out, let us know how you feel, and trust yourself to be strong. You've got this."

Turning her hand to clasp Amethyst's, Kat said, "You make me cry, I'll end up looking like a raccoon." The pep talk was one she hadn't even realized she needed.

In the back seat—her presence shielded from the two women—Estelle felt tears run down her own face. Brushing them away, she slowly let down the barrier and released a small boost of energy, causing the door buzzer to sound. She needn't have bothered. Both women felt her there as soon as the shield began to fall.

Amethyst eyed the ghost in the rearview mirror, "Hello, Estelle. What brings you out on this fine night? Have you been eavesdropping long?" While Kat swiveled as far as the seat belt let her.

"Popped in to provide a little moral support, but I can see you don't need me." She sniffed a little, then turned to Kat, "I'm so proud of you."

"For doing what? My life has mostly changed for the better because of you. All I did was let you talk to Julie."

Kat remembered the day Estelle had just barged in and taken over. She'd been so scared and then amazed because she had seen the world, even if through the eyes of a ghost, for the first time in years. "Technically, I didn't even do that much since you never asked permission."

"I've apologized for that." Estelle had the decency to look chagrined.

"Well, stop it. If you had, I would have run like a scared rabbit, and nothing would have changed. You've inspired me to be more impetuous—which is why, tomorrow, I'm going car shopping. How's that for moving forward?"

Amethyst got misty-eyed for a second time. Estelle and Julius had a profound impact on her own life. Thanks to their meddling, she and Reid had gotten a second chance at making their marriage work. Catching Estelle's eye in the mirror, she mouthed thank you and watched as the spirit brushed away a tear and faded from sight.

"Are you meeting Zack here tonight?"

"No, why? No. There's nothing going on between us."

Now that was a bet Amethyst could finally win. "He'll be here."

"I doubt it."

"Ten bucks says he will. Ten more says you'll dance with him."

"I can promise that's not going to happen, so even if he shows, I'll break even. You're on."

"This looks nothing like I imagined it," Kat shouted to be heard over the sheer volume created by two very drunk men singing a nearly unrecognizable rendition of "We Will Rock You."

Hanging lights dimly illuminated booths and tables in great contrast with the harsh spots that fell on the small stage and glinted off the shining chrome rings of the drum kit.

Somehow, the room seemed both smaller and larger than she had expected, as full as it was with laughing people. The sharp tang of beer and bodies overheated from a turn on the dance floor assailed her nostrils the same way it always did but being able to see the press of humanity made the experience richer.

Making an effort not to seem too eager, too new, Kat finally pasted what she hoped was a good approximation of a bored expression on her face and sat back to sip something fruity that barely tasted alcoholic in nature.

During the first break, Kat lost her first bet with Amethyst when Zack walked up behind her and greeted everyone at the table. Somehow, in all of the scooting over, he ended up seated right next to her, and she just knew Gustavia had maneuvered her again.

His obvious effort to keep from touching her was so distracting she forgot she'd passed her normal limit of two drinks and was just starting on her third when Gustavia grabbed her arm and shouted, "We're up next," into her ear.

"Oh, okay." Her toe caught in the rung of the chair as she stepped from the table, and she nearly stumbled until Zack reached out a steadying hand.

Face flaming red, she mumbled, "Thanks," and followed the others to the stage where embarrassment forgotten, she accepted the bass from a man she had met several times before but had never seen before and flung the strap over her shoulder.

Gustavia launched into the first riff of Barracuda, and Kat nearly missed her cue. Nothing felt exactly as it should. Not her hand on the neck of the instrument or the placement of her fingers on the strings. Finally, she closed her eyes, and that did the trick. She had learned to play by feel rather than by sight, so the darkness brought her back to the familiar.

When Julie launched into the first notes, Kat's eyes popped open. She wanted to watch. The distraction of seeing the performance was enough to make her forget her earlier awkwardness and finally lose herself in the music.

Until she caught sight of the crowd. All those eyes. Staring Watching. Her stomach flipped and then flopped. A cold sweat broke out on her forehead. Kat closed her eyes again to connect with the music and block out the onlookers. This must be stage fright.

No matter what Gustavia said, picturing an entire bar full of half-naked people would not make her feel better. That was one thing she never doubted.

Her hands were shaking by the time the song ended. Cries of "more" quickly turned into a chant. Gustavia called out, "Kat, don't you want to sing?"

Now there was a lump in her throat that felt like a rock. Swallowing twice in rapid succession, Kat shook her head. What was the deal? She'd sung on this stage plenty of times. Tonight, however, she'd be lucky to eke out a squeak.

"Let's do Little Bird next," Julie suggested.

Still unable to speak past the tightness, Kat nodded. Keeping her eyes tightly closed, she narrowed her focus to let in only the music and the lyrics. Her breathing slowed, the lump eased, and after a moment, she felt as though Annie Lennox, through Julie, was speaking straight to her.

From somewhere outside herself, a sense of warmth and acceptance fell like a warm blanket over her jangled nerves. It gentled and soothed.

It was her time to fly, her time to leave the nest. Kat opened her eyes, and this time the crowd had lost that menacing presence. Looking out, she saw smiling faces and happy people clapping along to the song, sending her positive energy.

Except for Zack, who sat with an odd expression on his face.

By the time the last notes faded away, Kat was enjoying the experience as much as she ever had, and this time, when the crowd asked for more, she decided to sing Black Horse and A Cherry Tree.

If she glanced over at Zack a few times during the chorus, well, it was nothing more than the truth.

He was not the one for her.

CHAPTER EIGHTEEN

Gustavia shot her brother a saucy wink as she shuffled chairs around, and he ended up sitting next to Kat. Not awkward at all, the thought as he angled himself as far away from her as possible. There were things he wanted to say, but this was not the place or time.

Relief washed over him when she got up to take the stage. He felt the jolt when her foot caught on his chair. Instinct took over when she stumbled. Unable to help himself, he reached out to steady her. Just that brief touch brought back the memory of kissing her.

He nearly groaned at the flood of emotions that memory brought with it. Desire, yes—but there was more. There was that same sense of anticipation he had felt as a child when Christmas came around, and he held a brightly wrapped package in his hands. Sure, it might turn out to be socks, but it might also be a robot or a toy car. Either way, it would be a delicious surprise—one he felt compelled to unwrap.

Zack pulled his mind back from that track—Kat was not a

gift to be unwrapped.

Stop. Just stop, he told himself.

Then she was playing, and when that moment of stage fright, of self-doubt, passed through her, he felt the sharp stab of it just as keenly. When her breath shortened and strained, the weight of it sank into his chest.

What was happening to him?

Tension mounted as her fear grew within them both. Every lurch of her heart answered in his until he could take it no more and reversed the connection. Now, instead of her fear swamping him, he was the one doing the sending. Reassurance, acceptance, and strength were what he poured through the connection until he felt the fear subside.

He turned burning eyes toward the stage and tried to figure out how to sever whatever tenuous hold she had on him. Seconds passed, and as the height of emotion leveled off, and he transitioned into cop mode, he understood that she'd done nothing intentionally.

Watching intently, he saw that her eyes neither sought him out nor avoided him. None of the markers that normally pointed toward deception was present. If she'd been sitting across from him in interrogation, the word innocent would be flashing through his head.

There was only one conclusion he could draw from that deduction. If she had not been reaching out to him, then he must have been the one who had infiltrated her psyche. He had been the interloper.

Okay, they had some kind of weird connection.

It meant nothing.

Of course, it meant something, but it didn't mean he had feelings for her. It just meant…he forced his mind away from this train of thought and focused back on the stage.

Gustavia. He would watch his sister perform and forget all

about Kat and her siren song.

Zack lied to himself, thinking he could have done it, too. He could have purged every memory of her from his mind, forgotten how the trill of her laugh warmed something inside him, ignored that place inside him that answered her like an echo winging through the mountains.

When she started singing straight to him about how he wasn't the man for her, all he could think was, *Oh yes, I am.*

Two spots of color rode high on Kat's cheeks when she stepped down from the low platform that served as a stage. Her eyes darted toward the table. The chair next to hers now sat empty.

She was thankful and relieved she didn't need to spend the rest of the evening ignoring him, even if some small part of her cried out that this was a lie. That same inner voice also insisted he had been behind that warm rush of reassurance that had gotten her through a minor on-stage meltdown.

Stopping along the way to accept compliments, Kat made her way across the room toward the short hallway leading to the restrooms. A few minutes of quiet would go a long way toward being able to regroup. It was a decision she instantly regretted when Zack stepped out of the door on the left.

Drawn to him like a magnet to steel but still wary, she tried to circle past without speaking, but he had reached his limit. Pivoting, he put himself firmly in her path.

"We need to talk."

Shoulders squared, Kat gazed up at him defiantly, "About what? We had a moment, it was nice, and now it's over. Nothing to talk about."

His short bark of a laugh startled her. "That's a lie."

A raised eyebrow and a smirk met her glare at being called a liar, "My famous cop instincts, remember?"

"Fine, we had a moment, it was more than nice, and then you acted like a jerk, and now it's over. You made me feel stupid. Rejected. Undesirable. I'm still mad at you. What do your precious instincts say to that?"

Truth. Especially the part about him acting like a jerk.

"I never intended...oh, never mind."

Without saying what he had intended, he reached out, pulled her against him, and slowly lowered his lips until only a breath separated them from hers. Unable to resist, she moved that fraction of an inch and felt the contact all the way down to her toes.

She might not have much basis for comparison, but the man stirred up her hormones with nothing more than a gentle touch of his lips.

Emotion washed over him. She tasted like a warm summer day, the kind you had as a kid when there were no responsibilities and the day—no, your entire life—stretched out ahead of you, rife with possibility, and everything seemed cleaner, clearer.

At that moment, he knew she was his future.

It wasn't supposed to be like this. She knew that even as his kiss washed through her like liquid fire igniting her to respond. Stupid hormones, what did they know?

How did someone who had never fallen know when they were in love? Because that's what this felt like.

Kat pressed closer, let him take the kiss deeper, and dived after him. For the second time in her adult life, she wanted to know what it meant to take that final step, to drop the barriers that had kept her from knowing what it meant to love.

When he pulled back just the tiniest bit, she whispered, "More," and dragged him back under until he broke the kiss and let his eyes search hers. Matching her gaze to his, she saw desire, tenderness, and things she didn't quite understand but wanted to.

"Kat, we need to stop now while I still can." He'd probably have to turn in his man card, but he didn't want to be her first foray into the world of physical love unless it was to take their relationship to the next level, and since he had no idea what level they were on now, it was best to put a stop to it while he still could.

"I'm not asking you to stop. Or don't you want me?"

He dragged her closer, proving how very much he did want her, and quirked an eyebrow at her to see if she'd gotten his point.

"Oh, I see. Then what?" This relationship stuff was harder than it looked, especially when she had to pick her way through it without much guidance.

"When we sleep together, I want it to mean something more than just satisfying your curiosity."

Kat pulled away from him to bang her palm on her forehead a few times before stalking outside into the cold air of a springtime night.

Zack followed and, while she ranted, installed her in his car and started it to get the heater working.

"Do you have any idea how incredibly frustrating this is? I went from passing notes with '*Do you like me? Check yes or no*' to being a full-grown adult with nothing in between. I've never had my heart broken, never had a boyfriend. Now I'm supposed to become part of the dating world, and I have no experience. I don't know how to act, what to say, what to do."

"Not to put down my gender, but what stupid men have you been around if none of them could see how incredibly special you are?"

That took the rant right out of her.

The window glass felt wonderfully cool on her cheek as she rested her face against it for a moment before telling him, "It was me. I decided my situation was too complicated to inflict on anyone else, so I avoided getting into a relationship. Blind is enough to take on. Blind and psychic was more of a burden than I ever wanted to be."

Sympathy flooded through him, then burned away like tissue in a flame, with a flare that left nothing but ash in the wind.

"Chicken."

"Excuse me?" Glaciers were warmer than her tone.

"I have to call it like I see it, and I'm not saying you were wrong to be afraid, but you chose to close yourself off, so you don't get to play the sympathy card."

Simple truth. Undeniable.

"But..." All the fight went out of her. "You're right."

"You're wrong about another thing, too. You did get your heart broken, just not by someone else." He paused to let his words sink in.

"My own worst enemy, so I am."

Zack chuckled, "Yoda wisdom, there's hope for you yet."

Kat smiled.

"Yes." He nodded as if she had asked a question.

"Yes, what?" Had she missed something?

"The answer is yes. If you passed me a note with the checkboxes on it, I'd check yes."

Kat smiled harder as he added, "I'd send you back a note asking you to go steady. Check yes or no."

"Yes."

"Okay, now that that's all settled, you need to know I'm not the kind of guy who puts out. At least until prom, but I might let you get to second base."

"Silly man. Take me inside and dance with me, then."

On the way past the table, she tossed Amethyst a twenty. Even breaking her winning streak couldn't pull the smile off her face.

CHAPTER NINETEEN

It was one of those movie moments where the hero—or heroines in this case—walk toward the battle in slow motion with the wind blowing through their hair. Except that wind apparently did not affect angels or ghosts.

Following the plan, once Julius announced it was time, Kat and Amethyst took their places in the gazebo while Galmadriel cast her shield over the structure.

Neither Logan nor the earthwalker would see them even though they sat in plain sight. Estelle left it to Tyler to alert the others and then took her favorite position on the roof to serve as lookout. Using another of Galmadriel's shields, Julius whispered in Logan's ear, subtly leading him toward the trap.

From her spot in the gazebo, Kat watched Julie and Gustavia move away from the safety of the house, ostensibly to clean up branches shed during harsh winter storms. Tuned in, as she was, to Julius' energy, she felt the cold darkness ease closer and closer as Logan crept silently through the forest.

She knew when he began skirting the edge of the tree line to position himself for the strike. She felt the chill created by the earthwalker as it advanced toward the gazebo, trembled as it shivered through her.

One look at Amethyst was enough to know she, too, felt the strain. Kat grasped the aura reader's hand. She felt a surge of reassurance run through the energy that made up Galmadriel's shield. The plan was working.

On cue, Logan stalked silently out of the woods without the first clue that Julie and Gustavia were aware of his proximity.

For one second, the true spirit of the man fought his way to the surface. Kat could see it in the ravaged look in his eyes, the twist of his face into a silent scream that Billy, the earthwalker, quickly subdued. She shivered again when his eyes turned black.

The plan had sounded reasonable, even simple when they were formulating it, but now that she was finally face-to-face with Logan, it felt impossible. Would she be able to give Billy that last chance? Convince him to go into the light? And what if she failed? What would happen to Logan then? No matter what he had done, he deserved to be free from Billy's influence.

That was the thought that haunted Kat as Logan unknowingly stepped into Galmadriel's circle, and the game was on.

Impending sunset painted a watercolor of pale pinks and oranges across a delicate, spring-chilled sky while the pungent smell of mud rose from earth in the early stages of thaw.

Estelle watched from her hidden vantage point as Logan crept up on what he thought was an unsuspecting Gustavia who stood some distance away. If he had seen the way her eyes lit in anticipation, Logan might have steered clear of the woman whose body was already tensed for battle.

It would have saved him a butt-whooping. Instead, he moved

closer and then reached out to grasp her by the shoulder.

With speed gained by some extra training since their last encounter, Gustavia used the element of surprise as she whirled, grabbed his arm, and pulled him hard into her bent knee, and when he staggered back, followed up with an uppercut to the jaw.

Breath wheezing, Logan pulled himself upright, and even though she saw the short jab coming, Gustavia couldn't fully dodge the blow. Her head snapped back as he tagged her hard enough to bring tears but not hard enough to take her out of the fight.

Instead, the blow just fueled her deadly calm, and she retaliated with a left hook and then stepped in to tromp on his instep. She knew he outmatched her in size, but this time, she had tenacity and preparedness on her side. He took a step back to gather himself for a kick, but Gustavia got there first, landing her boot-laden foot squarely between his legs with all the force she could muster. He went down with a groan, clutching himself and gasping.

Hands on hips, Gustavia stood over Logan as he lay on the ground, her chest heaving from a combination of exhilaration and exertion. Scraped skin on both sets of knuckles stung and burned, blood dripping from the split lip, but she barely noticed.

Taking him down might wander into payback territory, but she refused to feel bad about it. Instead, she congratulated herself for suppressing the intense desire to kick him a few more times and stalked over to where the others clustered around Galmadriel.

A wicked glint in her eye, she pointed to Kat. "Your turn."

Kat kept one eye on the man still curled into a fetal position, the faint shadow of the entity inside him clearly visible to her psychic eye. A wave of compassion washed over her to compete with the satisfaction of having watched Gustavia get a bit of her own back.

It was a complex situation; this man had spent most of the past year terrorizing people she loved, and part of her felt that he deserved the horror of being an unwilling vessel to an earthwalker. She was not proud of so petty an emotion.

"Billy," she called out to the shadow. "We are giving you one chance to leave willingly. You can still go into the light but only by choice. That option will not be open if we have to force you out."

In response, Billy leered. "Screw you, bi…"

Galmadriel gestured and, with the flick of a finger, set a ring—a prison—of white light to surround the still twitching form before turning back to the group of women.

"He has made his choice. Shall we begin?"

Zack spun the wheel, gunned the engine, and accelerated into the final curve. "Hang on, almost there." He spoke to the other three men in the car with him, his sister, and Kat.

Fear twanged at nerves taut as guitar strings while his intuition screamed, "Danger." When he got hold of them, all four women would answer to him for their part in what he knew was happening at this very minute.

He'd given in to the idea that the women would become the focus of this little supernatural sting but not that it would happen with none of the men present. Worse, Gustavia had lied so smoothly she'd skimmed right past his defenses.

"Take Finn out and get to know him. He's going to be part of the family soon. Maybe Tyler and Reid would like to go along. Play some pool."

So he'd gone, and look what happened the minute his back was turned.

Mixed with anger and fear, chagrin at being duped reddened

his face and fed the glut of emotions. Foot jammed on the brake; he skidded the cruiser into place, shoved the shifter into park, and was out the door almost before it came to a complete stop.

With Tyler, Finn, and Reid right behind him, Zack rounded the corner of the house and bolted toward the source of the light, his heart beating so hard it sounded like a metronome.

What he saw when he got there stopped him in his tracks. A huge dome of light, generated by the angel's outstretched arms, arched across the flat lawn, still covered with dead winter grass. From her eyes, twin beams of light converged into one shaft of pure white that grew to encompass the man Zack had been hunting for all these months.

Pinned by the light, Logan lay in the center of the circle, surrounded by the four women Zack had come to protect, and it looked like they didn't need him at all.

Zack felt the tingling sensation when every hair on his body lifted and stood on end as though touched by static electricity, felt a humming start to vibrate at the back of his throat. He swallowed heavily and glanced over at his future brother-in-law only to see the same grim expression on Finn's face that he was sure was pasted on his own.

The air around Zack crackled and sparked as the sharp tang of ozone flared his nostrils. Logan snarled, Billy's face superimposed over his own, and gathered the darkness to pit it against the light. Inky blackness formed closely around him. It was enough to let him pull himself up from the ground. Slowly, head bowed with the effort, Billy raised Logan's body to its knees.

Zack knew he had to do something to help, but he only managed one step forward before Galmadriel's sharply barked command stopped him.

"No." She spared him little more than a glance, but Zack had no choice other than to obey when the angel spoke directly into his mind, "This is not for you."

Billy sneered and spoke, "Not much of an angel, are you? Getting a bunch of women," the word was spoken as an epithet, "to do your dirty work."

"Want me to kick him in the danglies again?" Gustavia asked. Galmadriel spared her a smile, barely a quirk of the lips.

"Not much of a specter, are you?" Kat allowed scorn to color her words. Billy was more likely to lose his hold on Logan if he lost control of his emotions. "Getting a mortal to do your dirty work. I guess you didn't have it in you to go up against an angel and a bunch of women on your own."

Goading Billy might make him withdraw from the not-quite-innocent man whose body he now controlled. "But then, you've always been a coward, haven't you? A sneak, a cheat, and a liar. You will not win. Your kind never does." The words spat like knives—aimed at his ego—slapped at his control, pushing Billy past the edge of anger. They needed him off balance, and he was heading there fast.

Once they had Billy distracted, the real work could begin.

For Galmadriel's plan to work, each woman needed a strong reason to help Logan. Considering his actions before and after Billy had taken him over, finding that desire was a challenge.

The blackness in his heart had been the very thing that had created enough fertile ground for the earthwalker to plant his seeds. Having an ancestral connection to Billy only made his hold over Logan all the stronger.

To get herself into that mindset, Julie cast her memory back to the early days of their relationship. She found it difficult since the past was now colored by the knowledge that he had cold-bloodedly selected her as an easy target, a mark. For that and for everything he had done to hurt her since, forgiveness seemed impossible.

"Even the most hardened criminal can earn redemption. There were times when he showed you the spark of his truest self. Find that spark and use it." Galmadriel's words evoked a slide show of memories that flowed with enhanced clarity through Julie's mind.

There had been a moment on their third date when he had gone quiet, serious. Maybe it had been a ploy; maybe it had been a genuine emotion when he had said to her, "I don't deserve to be involved with someone like you."

At the time, she had found his self-deprecation flattering, but in hindsight, she knew he had, at that moment, spoken truly and that the regret in his eyes had been real.

Clinging to that memory, Julie allowed herself to fill up with the desire to nurture the tarnished pieces of his soul into something bright and shining. Golden light filled her inside, then spread from her to mingle with the purity of Galmadriel's brilliant whiteness and arrowed toward Logan.

The biggest surprise came when she felt an answering glimmer. He was still in there somewhere. She poured everything into helping the man she had once known so he could push back against the force inside him.

Even swallowed up by the earthwalker, Julie was aware when Logan responded with gratitude.

Billy shrieked his rage, an inhuman sound that produced the same reaction as nails on a chalkboard—a house-sized chalkboard and the nails the size of a dragon's claws.

Gustavia had no good memories of the man; she had known from day one that his intentions were hurtful, even if she had not been able to make Julie believe. He could burn in hell for all she cared.

Yet, at Galmadriel's suggestion, she remembered how in the one moment he had come back to himself, Logan had shown

154

remorse for kidnapping her and asked for help. The innate generosity of her nature would not deny the most basic of human emotions. Sympathy.

Under the intensity of the angel's gaze, Gustavia rolled her eyes and found enough compassion to bring forth her own light. Blue as a robin's egg, clear as the sky, it sparkled toward the man who had hurt her as she tossed a thought toward Galmadriel, "I better get huge karma points for this."

For Amethyst, the process was easier. Regardless of the pain he had caused, Logan had been directly responsible for the circumstances that led her to embrace the highest level of her ability. If for no other reason than the elevated desire to help that came along with being a true reader, she found her light. Appropriately colored, violet, and deeply intense, it flared through her and into the mix.

Logan's body shuddered and bucked as Billy's darkness swelled briefly.

Kat needed no prompting. Channeling Estelle that first time, the ghost had not asked permission, so Kat knew the terror that came with losing control. Whatever Logan had done, Billy's intentions were far worse. Let Zack and the legal system handle Logan's well-deserved punishment, Billy would answer to a higher court. She dropped her shield and added the brilliant green of new summer grass to the light flowing into the circle's center.

"By our light, we anchor this man to the earth and bind the darkness."

Outside the circle of light, a funnel of wind spun and grew around the women as if they were pulling energy from the very air. Dead leaves, grass, and twigs rose to whirl into the deepening twilight to be eaten by the frenetic rush of air and energy.

"It's not going to be enough. Look." Zack pointed. Instead of pulling the darkness from Logan's body, the shaft of light was being absorbed slowly by the earthwalker. He felt Galmadriel's attention leave him as she focused more and more of it on channeling the light into the growing void.

"What do we do?" Reid asked.

"When she was searching for Gustavia, we helped Amethyst increase her power by touching her. Maybe the same thing would work now," Tyler shouted over the howling wind. If they waited much longer, it would be impossible to get through that barrier.

"It's worth a shot. Let's go." The four men turned to fight their way toward the women who stood untouched by the maelstrom around them.

Spreading out around the dome of light, each man stepped into the flying debris pitched by the raging wind. They felt its force pulling at them with an almost sentient hunger.

Zack quickly realized how much damage a twig could do at high speed when one whizzed across his earlobe, then continued on its path with a bit of his skin attached. Bent nearly double, he yanked his coat over his head and leaned harder into the battle but made no headway as the wind stole his breath and tried to force itself into his pores.

A glance told him the others were faring no better, so he motioned them to pull back, to gather away from the mini tornado.

"Waited too long. It's too strong," he gasped with depleted breath.

"Then we work with it."

"How do you mean?" Reid asked.

Finn had a plan. "Don't try to cut across. Put the wind to your back and run with the flow. Work your way around the circle toward the middle."

Tyler nodded. "We need to go now. It's getting stronger."

Zack sprinted into the gathering storm, but this time he let the wind push him around the circle as he slowly angled toward the center. When he finally dropped out the other side, he saw the plan had worked.

Everyone had made it through. They stood between the dome of light and the howling storm.

He circled a hand to indicate they should all spread out around the circle of women. None of them knew whether they could pass the barrier of light, but when Zack gave the signal, they walked, without hesitation, into air chilled by the reaction of two opposing forces and by the entity contained at the center.

CHAPTER TWENTY

Billy, the earthwalker, felt the balance shift. He was winning, all he needed to do was hold out a little longer, and those pathetic women would be too tired to fight anymore. That knowledge lent him more power. The power to pull the muling body he now occupied up to standing.

With his attention fully focused on the angel, he did not see the men stumble into the light.

It is working, Galmadriel thought as she let her light go just a bit dimmer. He believes he is winning. Earthwalkers—their egos are always their downfall. She pasted a concerned look on her face knowing Billy would assume weakness and expend most of his power in what he thought would be a killing blast.

Having always walked with darkness, he did not understand the power of light. Or the universal law that what you send out will come back to you times three. Her plan was simple. Any schoolchild who had ever used the old comeback, "I am rubber, you are glue," would understand exactly what would happen next.

Still, it required utter focus and precision to emit exactly enough light to counteract his darkness but no more. In fact, these women were sending so much more than she needed that dimming her own was not only meant to deceive the Earthwalker but also to maintain the balance. Too much could set off a boomerang effect with dire consequences.

It was her own mistake that cost her. In maintaining the needed concentration level, she forgot about the four men ranging outside the vortex she had created to contain both light and dark energy.

Delight filled her as she watched Billy pull himself up—almost ready—so sure of his triumph yet so woefully outmatched. He gathered himself. She prepared to counter. He did not disappoint. He threw everything he had toward her; she caught his power with her own and began to feed light into his darkness.

That was the moment when she felt hands grasping hers and lost control of everything.

Zack stepped between Gustavia and Kat. Looking around, he saw the others taking their places, with Tyler between Julie and Galmadriel.

Nothing changed.

Billy now stood in the center, spewing venomous words at the angel whose light was slowly dimming.

Zack nodded to the other men, and all three reached out to grasp the hands of the women on either side of them.

Galmadriel screamed, "No," but it was too late. At the touch of Tyler's hand, a tremendous wave of power shot through her as each man added his color of light to the blazing shaft. Zack's light was red. Orange came from Tyler, while Finn offered deep indigo, and from Reid came the palest of pinks. He fully expected to be teased about it later.

Three things happened simultaneously. The windstorm they had created stopped. Just ceased its fury, twigs and leaves froze in the abruptly stilled air and then dropped to litter the ground in a perfect arc.

With a mighty boom, Billy was sucked out of Logan as if by a cosmic vacuum cleaner and yanked, screaming, into a pinpoint of nothingness. A loud zipping noise cut off the last of his shrieks.

Without making a sound, Kat slumped to the ground.

CHAPTER TWENTY-ONE

"Gustavia, go check on Kat." Keeping one eye on her crumpled form, Zack choosing duty while trusting his sister to care for his heart, split off to deal with Logan. Tyler followed Zack in case their quarry made any further trouble.

Crying and begging for mercy, Logan had no fight left in him. It was only the work of a couple of minutes to get him into restraints, read him the revised Miranda, and stash him safely in the backseat of Zack's cruiser.

Something is wrong with Kat.

Kat might have called it sensitivity, he considered it intuition, but both of these terms were little more than semantics. Something was wrong, and Zack knew it with a certainty that had his heart hammering in his chest and lent speed to his feet.

Gustavia, her face a mask of concern, was the first to reach Kat, where she lay unmoving on the grass. A breath-stealing dread settled over Amethyst, who was only a step behind. From what she could see, Kat no longer had an aura, and in her experience, that could only mean one thing the very worst

161

had happened.

She was gone.

Falling to her knees beside Kat's prone body, Gustavia reached out a trembling hand to check for a pulse. It was there, steady and strong.

"She's alive."

Courtesy of their timer, the fairy lights strung along the eaves of the gazebo flickered to life in the cooling darkness, their twinkling lights cheery but providing very little illumination.

When Julie spoke in her ear, Amethyst left Gustavia with Kat and strode over to where Galmadriel knelt on the grass, her body hunched as if she might be praying.

Filled with concern for Kat, Amethyst only spared enough attention to notice the light normally emanating from the Angel was so greatly reduced that her face was no longer visible. Still, there was no time to be concerned about what that might mean.

"Help her. There must be something you can do." Amethyst reached out to grab Galmadriel's arm but thought better of it. Being on the bad side of an angry angel once was a lesson learned for life. She snatched her hand back.

A closer look told her Kat might not be the only one needing help. This time, when her hand reached out, it was with the right intention, and she cleared what she could, as quickly as possible, from the weakened aura.

"Go," Galmadriel's voice was hoarse, "take Kathleen inside. I will be along presently."

Zack and Tyler had jogged back to where the entire group gathered around Kat. "Let's get her inside." Zack bent to scoop the unconscious woman into his arms.

With every step toward the house, his gut screamed a little louder that something was very, very wrong. Kat's body felt boneless. Gently he lowered her to the sofa and then glanced back over his shoulder to see his shock and despair echoed in every pair of eyes save one.

Galmadriel's face was blank, glazed as though she was tuned in to something none of them could see.

"I can't see her aura. It's like she's not there anymore." Amethyst said again to Galmadriel.

"In the backlash of extra power, her soul followed the earthwalker when he left this plane of existence."

Fury washed over Zack at her words. "Just what does that mean? Is she dying? Did we send her to a dark place?" He thrust a hand through his hair until it stood wildly on end. "We have to get her back. Tell me what to do." His voice rose until it sounded unnaturally loud in the room.

"Silence." Galmadriel's command sounded equally harsh. "If you had listened to me in the first place, this would not have happened." She paused to let that bit of information sink in.

"There is a way, but we must hurry. Julius and Estelle, you will join me in creating a bridge to the other side. Amethyst, you will help your friends anchor that bridge in this plane. One of you must cross over to bring her back. There will be great risk involved and little time to dither. You must now choose who it is to be."

"I'll go. I've known her longest," Gustavia volunteered.

"No. I'll go. It has to be me. Don't you see? I love her, and I'll bring her back because I'm not sure I can live without her," Zack insisted.

"How long have you known?"

"Probably since I rescued her from that first date but two minutes ago is the first time I admitted it to myself. I need to tell her." Zack turned to Galmadriel.

"Tell me what to do. I'm ready."

"Follow your heart. It will not fail to lead you but heed my warning. If you tarry overlong, you will share her fate."

The angel reached out her hand and touched Zack gently on the forehead. His long lashes dropped to flutter against his cheek then Gustavia cried out as he sagged to the floor.

"Hurry now," Galmadriel spoke quickly to Amethyst. "Once I create the bridge, you will see its aura. Use your healing ability to hold it firmly on this side, to anchor it down for as long as you can. You will understand how. When you feel it standing strong, give him," she pointed to Zack, "a push in the correct direction." She waved a hand imperiously for Julius and Estelle to follow her then they all winked out of sight.

Face strained with effort, Amethyst waited until she saw a rainbow arching back from the point where the angel had been standing.

"Everyone stand right here," she pushed her friends into a loose semi-circle. "Don't move no matter what. I don't know what will happen, but you heard what she said. We could lose them both if we fail."

Using a series of rapid hand movements, the flicked the colors from the end of the bridge, linking them with the matching ones in her friend's auras, then pulled the ends of the rainbow through them, wrapping it around herself the way a climber might secure a rope to a tree.

When she felt she had as firm a hold as she would ever get, she grounded the light as deeply as she could to anchor it. Then Amethyst grasped Zack's aura and flung it toward the arc of the rainbow bridge. Now, all that was left for them to do was wait and hold tight.

CHAPTER TWENTY-TWO

When she felt Billy's touch, cold as bitter wind and fetid as rotting meat, just before her life force was wrenched from her body, Kat knew something had gone horribly wrong.

Darkness deeper than anything she had ever experienced fell over her while Billy shrieked until a mighty thunderclap burst against her ears, then washed away, taking all sound with it. Not even an echo remained. Was this what it felt like to die?

Something tickled Kat's nose. She brushed at it, automatically opening her eyes. Grass.

Thinking she might still be lying near the gazebo at Hayward House, Kat struggled to her feet and then turned in a circle.

She was alone. Utterly alone in a place where nothing was familiar.

There was no gazebo, no Hayward House in the distance.

Instead, an endless field of grass lit not by the sun but by an ambient light that came from everywhere and nowhere at the same time stretched in every direction.

Now what?

"Galmadriel?" Kat called out into the silent atmosphere. She could hear her voice, but it sounded strange like it never left her to travel in normal waves.

If this was the afterlife, it wasn't living up to her expectations. No tunnel, no bright light, no crowd of loved ones waiting to welcome her home. So much for preconceived notions.

Kat whirled in place again, then walked—well, since there was no sun to be seen, she had no idea in which direction—forward. Everything was utterly still. No breeze brushed the grass into motion or whispered through the blades. The quiet unnerved her nearly as much as the sound of her earlier shout had done.

Though there was little enough to look at, Kat found that her vision was clearer than it had ever been. Looking down at a blade of grass, she could see every tiny ridge, every variation of color. Greens so vibrant they very nearly appeared to be unreal speared toward her, toward the light.

Bending down, Kat pulled off her shoes and left them behind to race barefoot through the verdant field of uninterrupted green. She relished how it felt to run without being on a treadmill, looking behind her to see the grass spring back up, erasing every spot where her feet had crushed it down. With that joy in her, Kat arced through the air, leaping and creating her own breeze until darker emotions crept in to edge out the happiness.

Tears streamed down her cheeks. Could this be all that was left to her? Running alone through some otherworldly place with no chance to say goodbye to her family, her friends, to Zack. The fleeting joy could not compete with that sadness.

Wasn't your life supposed to pass before your eyes? Like a movie—that's how people who had had near-death experiences described it. No reel played for her, no review of her decisions, good or bad. No eternal record of her regrets or accomplishments, and she had some of both. She should have chosen to trust. Should have realized love could overcome such petty obstacles as blindness or psychic ability. Should have understood neither of those things defined her or branded her as less. She should have told Zack she loved him.

Breath coming faster now, Kat pulled the sparkling air into her lungs and felt its clarity lend even more speed to her feet. She ran without tiring but eventually, with nothing to run toward but more of the same, she stopped and stood still again.

Glancing down, she saw her shoes.

Seriously? What was this? The cosmic version of a treadmill?

Behind that thought came the certain knowledge that though she could not seem to go forward or back through this place, she could, if she chose, move on to the next. Kat was also certain there would be no going back if she did.

Kat stood, frozen with indecision.

That was where Zack found her.

It had already been a weird enough day that the novelty of running along a rainbow didn't even register on Zack's strange-o-meter. There was no trail or sign of Kat or her passing until he took that last step across the arching bridge.

Looking around in surprise, he found himself standing in front of a landscape that looked very much like his own painting. Dreary gray buildings splashed with darker shades under a thundercloud sky, not another person in sight.

Kat, where was she? He lifted his head the same way Lola might when she was learning the scent of a thing.

He turned to see Julius, Estelle, and Galmadriel working to hold down their end of the pathway back. Seeing them struggle, he could tell their ability to continue was limited. Zack walked away from the bridge while marking its position in his memory. The last thing he wanted to do was forget the way back.

"Kat. Can you hear me?" Zack called out. His voice, swallowed by the vastness of the shimmering distance, didn't even echo off the structures. He ran straight ahead, marking each building for what felt like only a few minutes, but somehow knew time in this place might turn around on itself.

What was it she had asked him during their first dance? Did he believe in intuition? Maybe she had sensed something more in him right from the start. If there was anything remotely psychic about his cop sense, now was the time to find out. Zack stopped, stood still, and closed his eyes to imagine her, to use that memory to connect with the gut feeling he had always trusted. It was there. A tiny spark of knowing.

Left, she'd gone that way. He turned and fed the spark with trust until it burned into a steady flame. She was moving slowly away from him; he could feel the distance between them lengthening. Zack broke into a run.

"Kat. Kat. Kat," he chanted her name with each beat of his feet on the pavement. The flame became a beacon, a flare that he sent along ahead to carry his need for her, his love.

Left, then right. By now, he had forgotten to count the buildings. Getting back had become less important than finding her.

"Kat." He called louder with both heart and voice.

There, he could see something now. A faint, small shadow some way ahead.

He thought he heard her shout, "Hello."

Then she was gone again. He put on more speed, panting now, stretching his limits.

Around the next corner, he roared to a stop. It was her, facing away from him just like the boy in his painting—the one he'd never told anyone was him.

Instead of a teddy bear, she held a pair of running shoes in her hand.

"Kat, I'm here." She heard him.

"Zack?" Kat stopped. She felt as though she had been running for hours. Maybe she had. Turning, she saw him coming toward her and raced to meet him.

He scooped her into his arms to rain kisses across her face. "I found you. Never leave me again."

"I didn't mean to...everything was all whirling, and then I ended up here knowing I would probably never be able to go back. All I could think about was how much I would miss you. And that it was time to move on."

Before she could speak, he scooped her up to carry her back the way he thought he had come, the way that would lead him back to the bridge, but something in her voice stopped him.

"Is that what you want? To move on?"

"I don't think I can go back. I tried, and nothing happened. Why did you come? What if you can't go back? You shouldn't be stuck here because of me."

He bent his head to kiss her. "I couldn't let you go. I love you. Don't you want to go back? To be with me?"

"Of course I do. That's all I want because I love you, too."

"Very touching, but we cannot hold this bridge forever." Galmadriel's voice sounded breathless and very close. How had he run for miles and only been a few steps from where the angel stood?

"Go. Now."

Zack lowered Kat to her feet, grabbed her hand, and pulled her along with him. With each footfall, the colored light they crossed felt less substantial. That observation baffled Zack, but there was no time to rest or think about anything but getting her back where she belonged, back into her own body.

He spared no thought for whether his own lay vacant beside

hers. Getting her back would be enough, even if he didn't make it himself.

Rounding over the rainbow's curve, it was downhill now, so they put on more speed to race full out. The footing was so much less solid that now it felt like running through sand or deep water. Almost there, he could see Amethyst struggling to hold her end of the bridge in place.

The next thing he heard was Galmadriel's voice ringing in his ears. "Now," she commanded, and he felt Kat gathering herself for the leap. In the end, he wasn't sure if they jumped, fell, or were thrown but the last thing he remembered was the feeling of his feet tangling in something and seeing his body loom closer.

CHAPTER TWENTY-THREE

Letting a mortal go back once they had crossed over was against all the rules, but Galmadriel thought she could get away with it since Kat's body still lived. With all the grace she could muster, she decided to intervene because these were unusual circumstances. She could not stand by and let the woman die when her failure sent Kat across in the first place.

Clinging and fighting to anchor her end of the bridge, she felt it when Estelle and Julius began to fade; with energy flagging, neither could hold out much longer.

With their help, this plan had been tenuous at best. Without it, her oversight may now cost two lives instead of one.

Time slowed as she saw Kat and Zack nearing Amethyst. "Help them," she shouted toward the healer before the two spirits lost their grip on the bridge. Galmadriel strained to put everything she had into holding firm, and then she felt Zack's feet catch and pull. Pull her back toward the earthly plane.

Despair washed over her in that split second. She had failed everyone.

And, her light fading to nothing, the angel Galmadricl fcll.

CHAPTER TWENTY-FOUR

Kat felt something warm and wet slide up her cheek. Once then twice. She pried open an eye and tried to figure out what she was looking at. The warm, moist, pink thing approached again, accompanied by the unmistakable odor of Lola breath.

All she could think of was pushing the snuffling snout away from her face, but neither arm would move when she tried. Something bad must have happened because it felt like a huge weight rested on her chest. An accident, maybe?

Everything fell away again for a while. She didn't know how long, and then Lola was back. This time Kat groaned, "Lola, go on." Her voice felt raspy, like she'd been screaming for hours.

When she opened her eyes this time, she could see why her arms wouldn't move. Zack's chest lay half across her own, the steady rise and fall of his breathing a comfort, but his weight had her pinned to the floor. No, not the floor, someone's legs. They were all sprawled across the floor like bowling pins.

It took a minute before she remembered exactly what had happened. A stirring off to one side had her slanting her eyes over just in time to see Finn sit up with a mutter. Apparently,

Lola was making the rounds.

"Finn, help me." Kat tried to shove Zack's dead weight off her chest. "Is everyone okay?"

"I think so." He checked on Gustavia first, then, reassured by her even breathing, reached over to help Kat extricate herself from the pile. "That was intense." He pressed a hand to his temple, where a headache beat against his palm.

Julie, Reid, and Gustavia came to at about the same time, with Tyler not far behind. A minute later, Amethyst stirred, but when Zack woke up, it was not the soft, subtle process it had been with everyone else. He went from unconscious to hyperalert, leaping to his feet, eyes wide with concern.

Seeing Gustavia and Kat sitting together went a long way toward calming him down again. By then, Finn had located the downstairs bathroom and a blessedly large container of painkillers. He detoured to the kitchen for as many bottles of water as he could carry and returned to pass them around the room.

Despite the pounding in his head, Zack insisted on checking his prisoner. Finding Logan sprawled out in the still-locked cruiser, sound asleep relieved more of the headache than the painkillers could.

He pulled out his phone to call it in and discovered that his phone was either dead or destroyed due to whatever energy the angel had raised. He went back inside to use Julie's landline.

Within minutes, a deputy arrived to take charge of the prisoner. Zack would have to go in later and write up a detailed report, but that would have to wait until he decided what that report should say.

Meanwhile, Ellis would be booked and treated to a bed and a hot meal.

Duty over for the next little while, Zack went back inside.

Kat stepped back from the window, went to the door, and met Zack halfway down the drive. At first, her steps were uncertain. What if everything she remembered from her time on the other side had been a dream? Even now, it was fading like dreams do when touched by the light of morning.

When he looked up and saw her, she knew he'd been thinking the same thing.

"Was it a dream?" She had to know.

"It feels like it, but no, I'm sure it was real."

"So everything you said…"

"True, every last word of it."

Forgetting that he might still be shaky on his feet, she launched herself into his arms and clung there while he kissed her as if he would never stop. When he finally pulled back, Kat smiled into his eyes and asked, "What exactly is second base on a guy, and how long until Prom? I think I heard something about a five-date rule. How many dates have we been on?"

CHAPTER TWENTY-FIVE

Just before 10:20 am on the day of the spring equinox, the group assembled for the fourth and final time to watch Zack, the newest among them, slide the portrait of Julius into place. Julie closed her eyes and swallowed hard when it locked in with a soft click. In a few short minutes, she would have to say goodbye to Grams for a second time, and everything would change again.

Being the tallest, Gustavia still had to stretch to position five of the original ten glass lenses into the slots Kat had found. When it was done, she stepped back, reached blindly for Julie's hand. So much had happened over the past few months that this final search seemed sadly anti-climactic.

She glanced over to see Samantha bouncing in place, one of the prisms from the third search clutched tightly in her hand. This girl, her father; she marveled at how quickly they had become her life.

The sun would only strike the window for a limited time, so when Kat and Amethyst stepped forward with Sam to position the prisms, every key was in its place, ready for its light to play across the window and reveal the final clues.

It was a bittersweet moment.

Julie needed nothing more in the way of valuables. Never having been greedy, to begin with, her financial needs had already been so well met there was nothing left to do but pay it forward. To that end, Tyler and Reid were working to establish a foundation for young inventors, and she was confident they would make the venture a success. No matter what they found today, it would pale in comparison to the treasure of having friends who became family and the love of a man like her new husband, Tyler.

It was almost time for the first reveal. Eleven eager pairs of eyes watched as a beam of sparkling sunlight speared through the stained glass to make its way across the painting and illuminate a small, square section of library wall just above Julius' shoulder.

Standing next to Zack, Kat wished this day would never end. She was not alone.

She watched Julius for a moment, his body language more stiff and anxious than ever. All of this had been meant as a puzzle he hoped his son would one day be mature enough to solve. That it had never happened weighed on him almost as much as the danger he had unleashed in his zealous effort to provide the hidden items to Julie, the only family he had left.

Beside Julius, Estelle stood silently, her face settled into lines of misery, anticipating the pain of saying goodbye to her granddaughter for the second time. Julie wasn't the only one who would miss Estelle terribly when this day was over.

Busy thinking about upcoming goodbyes, Kat missed the moment when the sun passed through the window to land on the painting.

Gustavia approached the window with the second set of lenses in her hand. "We only need five of the ten pieces, so I say we start with the first five. Kat, you have the nimblest fingers. Come help me swap pieces until we get all the letters in place."

Only two minutes passed before the shaft of light flashed through the five lenses resting against the glass, lighting up the A, R, and H.

Working quickly, Gustavia swapped the highest lenses leaving the lower ones to Kat. With the second set of five settled into place, the sun picked out two more letters, T and E.

The pair stepped back to wait for what would happen next.

Again, Kat watched Julius as the light moved slowly toward the prisms. More agitated than ever, he made several exaggerated eye movements before she realized he was trying to communicate something. The third time he looked pointedly at the other window in the room, Kat got it and moved to close the curtains, darkening the room slightly.

Just as she turned back toward the window, light sliced through the glass to strike each of the three prisms. One directed a beam onto the painting to illuminate the number nine of the clock rendered with fine brush strokes behind Julius as he stood beside his desk.

A second beam arrowed across the room to land on the keystone of the arched fireplace. Long-legged Zack reached the spot first and called out, "Twenty-two. It's carved into the stone just there."

The third and final flare of light speared into the light fixture hanging in the center of the room, where it flashed into the etched glass star that was the central feature of what Julie had always considered the ugliest light in the house.

"And that would be a five, I presume?" Tyler grinned.

"Good thing we didn't pull that eyesore down and replace it."

"9-22-5."

All three clues in hand, the next step was to check out the spot in the library that corresponded with the painting. Shaking off the emotions that threatened to distract her again, Kat settled down with the other women to watch the men figure out how to access the secret area.

The four tapped, tested, poked, and prodded every nook and cranny of the trim surrounding the small spot. Finally, Zack reached out and simply shoved his hand hard against the flat panel. When it slid back and up, he turned with a broad grin and hoisted his fists in the air to indicate victory before stepping aside to let Julie take his place.

Already prepared, she pulled a small flashlight from her pocket to shine into the recess. A quick look had her passing the light to Tyler before reaching in to remove a box from the space, which she carried to the desk. Everyone gathered around to get a better look.

A complicated series of five small, lettered, combination lock dials formed a circle around a larger, numbered dial. The lettered dials spun easily, but the numbered one refused to move off zero.

Julie's dust-dry comment pulled a giggle from Kat, finally breaking some of the tension, "Overkill much?" As always, Julius was prevented from speaking until the search was completed. At his exaggerated scowl, some of the heavy atmosphere slid away.

"ARHTE? What kind of word is that?" Reid tried the combination in clockwise order, but nothing happened. "I'm assuming we have to dial in the correct outer combination before the inner dial moves."

"It's an anagram. Try earth," Amethyst suggested.

Reid spun the dials and spelled the word out. No dice.

"Heart?"

There was a soft click this time, and now the middle dial spun free.

Gustavia handed Julie the box. "Hurry up and open it."

The dial spun, and Julie felt the slight vibration as each tumbler locked into place. 9-22-5.

With no idea what might be inside, she slowly lifted the lid to see a stack of thin, leather-bound diaries. Flipping the first one open, she read her great-grandmother's name in flowing script.

"My mother's diaries." Finally freed to speak, Julius smiled at his great-granddaughter with affection. "She was quite a woman. You remind me of her." It was his highest compliment and delivered in a voice gruff with emotion. He had come to love this group of young people and hated to leave them, but it was time. Julius stepped back to let Estelle say her goodbyes.

Tears flowed from both ghostly and corporeal eyes as Estelle surveyed the room. "Take good care of each other." Then her eyes locked onto Julie's, "My love will be with you always, darling girl."

"And mine with you," Julie choked the words out and waited for the spirits to fade away.

And waited.

Nothing happened.

Estelle looked over at Julius, "I thought Galmadriel would be here."

"I haven't seen her since we brought Kat back across the bridge."

"Uh, Daddy?" Samantha felt it first, a prickle of energy that started at her toes and quickly worked its way up through her whole body, "Something's happening."

Before she finished her warning, everyone else felt the sensation, and a booming voice not unlike Galmadriel's filled the room. "Galmadriel has fallen. The pair of you caused this; you will work together now to fix it. She will be your first charge."

It seemed like everyone in the room gave a collected shiver as the sound faded away, taking most of the prickling energy with it.

"Why do I still feel...?" Julie trailed off as her attention became riveted to the spot where Julius and Estelle stood. Estelle raised one hand and slowly turned it in place, staring at it in wonder. Her hand and the rest of her glowed with light. An equally glowing Julius seemed less surprised. It appeared they had earned their angel status after all.

Estelle closed her eyes, concentrated, and the light faded to leave her looking more solid than ever. She turned to Julius and punched him as hard as she could in the arm. "I've wanted to do that since you talked me out of going into the light," then went to Julie and embraced her tightly to start the second round of goodbyes that included hugs for everyone.

CHAPTER TWENTY-SIX

Once the pair had finally gone, a long moment of silence threatened to turn maudlin until Amethyst, who was closest, turned to glance at the cavity where the box had been resting. A flutter of paper caught her eye.

"Jules, there's something else in here." It was enough distraction to pull the focus back to the present.

Finn stepped past Amethyst to reach in to pull out an envelope containing several folded sheets of paper, which he handed to Julie, who flipped open the first and scanned it.

"It's a dispensation allowing Julius to own several troy ounces of gold for use in creating his inventions."

"In 1933, the president signed an order making it illegal to own more than a small amount of gold without permission," Tyler explained.

The rest of the papers were gold certificates.

"You won't find it." Nine faces turned in surprise to see where this new voice had come from.

Julie recognized her from Estelle's pictures. "Mary Lou?"

"Yes." Mary Lou nodded.

"That gold is long gone, and those certificates? They're worthless."

Mary Lou was a woman of medium height with a long but gentle face.

"Arrogant man thought he was doing the right thing, keeping his wealth safe from his own son. Well, I knew all about that gold. Pried it out of those worthless clatter traps with his tools once I found where he'd stashed his plans."

"Behind the plaque in the kitchen," Julie breathed.

Mary Lou gave a savage nod. "Messing around in my kitchen and didn't think I would find out," she sniffed with disdain, "took some time, but I found his precious notebook with all his plans." She sneered. "Never found that dispensation paper, though. So we couldn't sell it through legal channels, but I found a buyer on the sly."

Had Julius known any of this? Kat didn't think so, and now she knew who had been whispering apologies into her ear every night that she'd stayed at Hayward House.

"Turns out Julius was right. Edward went through the money so fast I don't think Estelle ever knew he had it."

She shrugged the weight of confession heavy on her shoulders.

"But that wasn't as bad as what I did when I told that young man about the gold certificates."

The ghost dropped her head into her hands, her voice muffled, "I had no idea things would turn out the way they did. I thought I was helping." Mary Lou's head came up to show her face a mask of anguish.

"You have to know I only meant to help," she repeated, "figured maybe after all this time, those certificates might still be somewhere in the house and worth something. Maybe enough to fix up the roof, anyway. So I told your young man, the one who gave you all the trouble about the certificates. I was the cause of everything bad that happened to you."

"That jerk called me a whackadoodle, and he'd already seen a ghost?" Gustavia's voice seemed unnaturally loud in the silence that had followed Mary Lou's revelation, but her outraged exclamation broke the icy silence.

Kat snickered. Then Amethyst giggled, and before long, a smile tickled at the corners of Julie's mouth. Mary Lou sat patiently, watching as the young people slowly sank into a fit of laughter that left them breathless and clutching their sides.

When it had finally passed, Julie waved a hand at her great-grandmother and said, "You had no way of knowing, and it's all over now," She wiped away the tears laughter had sent streaming down her cheeks.

"I really am sorry."

Kat looked around the room, plenty of good had come from the events that Mary Lou had set in motion, and it was time for her to rest. "You're forgiven. Please, go back into the light. Find your son. We're all fine."

-The End-

Made in the USA
Las Vegas, NV
27 November 2023